MW00938310

Pleasure Extraordinaire

Pleasure Extraordinaire

3

LIV BENNETT

Copyright © 2014 Liv Bennett
All rights reserved.
ISBN-10: 1497577187
ISBN-13: 978-1497577183

All rights reserved, including the right to reproduce this book or portions thereof in any form whatsoever. The uploading, scanning, and distribution of this book in any form or by any means— including but not limited to electronic, mechanical, photocopying, recording, or otherwise—without the permission of the copyright holder is illegal and punishable by law.

This is a work of fiction. Names, characters, places and incidents are products of the author's imagination or are used fictitiously. Any resemblance to actual events or locales or persons, living or dead, is entirely coincidental.

Cover image © MarishaSha / ShutterStock.
Torn textured paper image on the cover © agencyby / Can Stock Photo Inc.
Swirl image © Can Stock Photo Inc. / Seamartini
Floral ornament image © Can Stock Photo Inc. / ThomasAmby

The dream I thought I was living in turns out to be the worst nightmare of my life. What Michael wants from me is more than posing as his girlfriend but he won't tell me why he hired me in the first place. I witness ugliness and abuse everywhere I turn. There is only one person who can rescue me from this hell.

Zane.

But he won't do it for free. Just like his father, he's out to take revenge and inflict pain. He holds the key to my freedom, and I'm ready to give him what he wants even if it means I'll hurt Ace in the process.

LIV BENNETT

The Way Out

Frustration, rage, and agony storm through my body as I pace down the hall toward the elevator, the sound of my high heels clacking on the marble floor echoing in my ears. I'm ensnared into a fictitious cage that's more restrictive than the state prison.

Desire to avenge and hurt someone is growing exponentially inside me. But more than that, I want it all to end. My suffering, the potential disasters that're awaiting my sister and me. And my life. It'd have been so easy if my life ended at this point. Was that what Michael's wife felt like before committing suicide? When she couldn't take it anymore, she just pulled the plug? If Michael pushed her, his own wife, the mother of his kids, to the edge of the proverbial cliff, only Heaven knows what he would do to me.

Michael wouldn't have this much power over me if it wasn't for the sex tape. And, that I owe it to Zane's able hands. Fury overcomes all the other emotions running havoc inside me and pushes my rationale into the depths of my mind. Zane's plan wasn't flawless, but his charm overcame the faults of his plot to get me where he wanted me. Helpless in his hands.

I could throw up the entire day, and it wouldn't empty the disgust churning in my body. However, I know a way that might possibly bring some balance to this horridly wrong equation.

The elevator doors open and close without me pushing for the call button, but I don't step in. Instead, I walk ahead until the end of the hall and rush through the doors of Zane's secretary's office. She shrieks in her seat at my sight, but I don't give her enough time to talk or ask me to leave. Zane's office doors slam open with a loud bang as I kick them.

Zane is talking on the phone, his feet propped up on his desk. The sickening smile freezes on his face as he notices my unannounced presence. He must see the depths of my anger, the reason I'm breaking into his office, where he's the king and the rest of us are worthless peasants, because he drops the phone onto his desk and rises to his feet in one swift move. His expression wouldn't be any less fearful if I entered with explosives wrapped around my body.

"Mr. Hawkins, shall I call security?" I hear his secretary speak and turn to see her at the doorway.

"Do that," I yell and push the door against her face. I might have had no intention of killing Macey Williams when I smashed her with my slap, but the idea of shedding Zane's blood, making him squirm with pain as I dig my teeth into his flesh is strangely welcoming. I leap the distance between us and grab him by the collar of his crisp white shirt. When I'm through with him, it'll take police investigators to discover the original color of his shirt.

"You." I glare at him to convey to him what

my tongue can't spell out. My whole body is trembling with the amount of anger that's new to me. Being fooled and used, humiliated and demeaned. And all were done intentionally. For what, I have yet to find out. "Mother fucker, bastard liar. You ruined me. You and your father. What did I do to you?"

"Lindsay, calm down. What's going on?"

"You're going to tell *me* what is going on." I'm broiling with the desire to hurt him, punch him in the face, kick him in the crotch, but my hands are too rigid around the collar of his shirt to move.

Lifting his hands cautiously to lay them on my wrists, Zane holds me in place. "Tell me what has you so angry."

How you lied to me in every aspect of your relationship with your father... How you played with my feelings... How you turned my body into a puddle of lust... How you used my weakness for you... And how I could believe it all...

"Tell me," he urges one more time, softly, as if he's worried about me. That does it for me, and I yank my hand out of his hold and smash it on his cheek.

Asshole player.

He quickly catches my hand, this time gripping both my wrists tightly. Satisfaction spreads over me as I stare at the traces of glowing red my fingers left on his face.

"The video tape," I say, forcing my hands away.

His eyes grow wide with shock. His mouth plops open, and I almost believe him. Almost.

"What video tape?" His sound is even more depressingly convincing than his alarmed expression. Honestly, where did he learn to act so well?

I shake my head in disbelief, turn around and head straight toward the exit. "The one you and your father used to trap me with."

I nearly collapse against the two large men, I guess security, at the doorway but quickly gain my composure and move around them before they can realize I'm the trouble they have to deal with. I run down the stairs without realizing it's a long way down, but I run anyway. Crying, yelling at myself, wiping away my tears. This shouldn't be happening to me. Where was my logic? My reason?

There must be a way out. I can't for the love of God let them use me like a silly toy. *Think, Lindsay, think.* Every puzzle has a solution. There has to be a way out of this too.

What's the worst possible scenario that can happen, and how can I avoid it?

Taylor. Yes. Being the reason for ending her career, her livelihood, and her future is enough to crash my soul after all she's done for me since my birth. She's been a mother, a father, a sister to me, and my best friend. But, her construction company is in danger because of me. If I can magically find a way to escape that predicament, I may survive this.

On the other hand, if such a solution doesn't exist, or I can't find it, I'll have to face indefinite humiliation in Michael's hands. He never mentioned a time limitation for our new *deal*. For all I know, I'm in it for a lifetime. Serving his associates and clients as a sex slave.

Finally, I reach the ground floor and pace out of the building that is home to the devil himself. I find my car in the parking lot. I'm not even sure if I should continue driving the vehicle I earned through the contract with Michael. But, I have no other transportation. After all their manipulations, I shouldn't obsess about being virtuous anyway, especially when Michael and Zane are anything but.

Although the reception in the parking lot isn't good, I dial Taylor's number. She doesn't answer. I try Adam's, and he picks up.

I force my voice to sound nonchalant and ask him how he is doing and how settling into their new home is coming along. He goes into detail about the remodeling of the kitchen and their furniture shopping, most of which I tune out.

When he at last inquires about the reason for my call, I ask him straight, "Did Taylor donate all her inheritance to charity?" After all, that is the crucial point in the survival of Taylor's company. If she's keeping her inheritance from her deceased first husband, she can save her construction company with those millions of dollars. And, even if the company can't be rescued, she will still have enough money to live in luxury.

"Bad news doesn't travel that fast. Yes, she did. About eight months ago. But only the part she received from Jack's father. She also had some from his mother, which wasn't a small sum by any means."

"Really. How much?" Shame isn't really one

of the assets I can afford these days.

"Why do you want to know?" Adam asks. "If you need money, I'm here to help too. It doesn't have to be a loan, either."

"No. I don't need money. Thanks anyway. You're the best bro-in-law one could ever have. I just want to know how much she has."

"Enough to live in luxury without having to work."

"Adam. Give me a number so I can come to that conclusion myself."

"Always obsessed with numbers, aren't you? A little over twelve million. And that doesn't include my own savings. We have enough for us, and for you too if you ever need help."

I gulp down the lump of shock in my throat and let the relief relax my overly tensed muscles. "Wow, Jack was indeed a jackpot for Taylor."

"I'll tell her you said that."

I laugh, now losing my senses all over again. "Oh, please do that. I'll finally have a reason to kick your ass."

Adam laughs too, recites me some details about Adriana, his sister, worthy the roll of my eyes, and invites me for dinner at their new home. I gladly accept, then hang up, and turn on the car engine.

Just when I maneuver the car out of the parking slot, Zane jumps in front of it. He rounds it and stands beside the door of the passenger's side, knocking on the window with his knuckle. I shake my head and press the gas pedal, ready to drive off, but he jumps on the hood of my car, and I'm forced to unlock the doors and let him in, although I'd gladly roll the car over his sordid body.

He straightens his suit and climbs in next to me. The cheek that had my slap seems redder than when I last saw it. Good.

"I have to apologize," he says.

"Really!"

"I never intended for Michael to get his hands on the video."

"Ahh, so you came after me to fool me into thinking that the video recording was for your personal enjoyment. Are you fucking kidding me?"

"That, too. But, that wasn't the main reason. I was planning to upload it online," he says calmly, as if those are the very words I need to hear to cool down.

My nostrils flare with renewed anger, and I tighten my fingers around the steering wheel so they won't do anything hurtful to him. Is he a fucking imbecile or just a sadist to tell me his plans straight up to my face?

"Listen." His entire upper body is turned toward me, his hands up, signaling me to calm down. "It was supposed to be for your own good, Lindsay. I wanted you to break free from Michael. I knew he'd demand more from you than you agreed to when you first signed the contract. He's after something big. I don't know what it is, but he wouldn't let you go any other way. That is why I had to put up the sex video for everyone to see, so there wouldn't be any reason for you to stay with him. He wouldn't be able to continue with the pretend relationship with you. He wouldn't be able to ask for the money back from you because you followed the rules of the contract to the last point. It'd be a win-win situation for you in every sense."

"And, I promise to everything good and holy, I was planning to ask you out and have you as my girlfriend for as long as you needed to so you don't appear as a whore to the public. It was a perfect plan, until Michael stole the video. I don't have any copies of it. If I did, I'd upload it online right away to save you. But, you can do it. You should do it. Tell him to fuck off and keep your money. It's not the end of the world if the video spreads around. You weren't really naked. No part of your body that you wouldn't show in public is seen in the video."

His features soften and he stares at me with affection. "And, I'll be with you. I promise. We can give press conferences and tell how madly we fell in love with each other and couldn't keep our hands off each other and all that nonsense. Your name will not be muddied. I'll marry you if it's what it takes to keep your dignity, but don't let my father use the video against you. Because that wasn't the main purpose of its production."

I let my mind absorb his words, slowly, enthusiastically. He's right. I wasn't naked while having sex, although I remember thinking it was strange. Although Zane could easily strip me naked, and it'd be his every right, he didn't. It indeed proves Zane's intentions while recording weren't to ruin my dignity. It wasn't like I was tied naked on a cross, my vagina, ass, or my breasts recorded up close while Zane is whipping me.

The cameras only recorded what they were

supposed to record. Zane and I having sex, nothing more, nothing less. Even though I appear completely undignified in that video, the media is bustling with much more obscene and degrading ones. "He's planning to upload the contract online as well."

"I read the contract, and really, it doesn't state anything tangible against you. If anything, it'll worsen his public image. I don't think he'll ever dare admit he is a homosexual in a million years. He won't do that. And, if he does, you'll have every right to sue him, because if you remember, confidentiality is a big part of that contract. You can literally destroy him if that contract gets into the hands of his competition. That'll be the end of him."

"Are you sure?" As much as I want to believe him, a part of me is snarling and saying no.

"Hell yes, I'm sure. I'm the very product of his fear that everyone will know he likes men to fuck him. I don't understand his fear, and I don't give a shit about it either. But, I can assure you, if he had to choose between dying and coming out of the closet, he won't hesitate to pick the former."

"I don't know. Why, then, did he threaten me with it?"

"He just knows how to control people. Must have used it to scare you shitless so you would comply without asking questions."

"Well, it *did* work."

What to do now? I won't push Michael's limits and yell into his face blatantly to go through whatever threats he has in store for me as Zane wants me to do, but I most certainly won't let it go so easily either. What he has done to me and is planning to do is criminal. No money in the world should give him the privilege to escape the punishment others would receive for the same act.

"So, are we good?" he asks.

I let out the breath I've been holding all this time and give him a weary smile. "I'm sorry I slapped you."

"Don't worry. It wasn't too bad, and I kind of liked it."

"Yeah, right."

"Hey, my marriage proposal is still on. It might not be the most romantic proposal, but I do promise to walk down the aisle with you to keep your name clean. Don't forget it."

"I'm not going to marry you, Zane. Forget it."

"That's not the reaction I was hoping to get."

"Sorry to disappoint, but I gotta go."

"What are you planning to do about Michael?"

"You'll find out soon enough, along with everyone else." I signal with my chin toward the door, and he climbs out obediently. As badly as I wanted to kill him a few minutes ago, I'm glad his intentions weren't sinister. I believe him. And I'll take the risk. Taylor won't be ruined as I feared. Although her construction company is her life, she won't end up on the streets like Michael claimed.

I hit the gas pedal, watching Zane through the rearview mirror, and maneuver straight toward the nearest police department.

After going through the security screening, an officer gives me a form and asks me to write down every detail related to the incident that I want to file a complaint about. It takes thirty-five minutes for me to pour out everything I remember onto the paper, from the contract and the video tape to Michael's homosexuality and his threat to upload the video and the contract online. I sign it and hand it back to the officer. She nods and tells me to wait until she registers it into the database.

I turn around and join the group of people waiting for their turns. As soon as the next one is called, I settle on the empty seat, unable to stop biting my nails. A pregnant girl in her early twenties walks past me between two officers. If it wasn't for the fact that her hands were handcuffed, I wouldn't think of her as a law breaker, because she looks clean and even sweet with her long blue shirt, skinny jeans, and flats. Her hair is tied up into a ponytail, and her face is deep pink and spotless. What must she have done to be arrested? Especially in her pregnant state. I can only think of stealing as the reason for her presence in the police station.

What will happen to her child if she has to stay in jail? Perhaps the close proximity of her age to mine makes me feel compassionate for her, but whatever crime she's committed, I don't think it's anywhere near as cruel as Michael's crimes, and he's free while this poor girl will probably give birth to her child inside the four walls of a state prison.

I glance up at the officer who took my case to see her talking to another officer, showing a paper, most likely my complaint, and looking toward my direction.

The officer she talks to simply nods, takes the document from the female officer's hand, and approaches me with a relatively angry expression on his face. I shouldn't let his gesture get to me, I think to myself. It must be his usual, everyday expression. He introduces himself as Lieutenant Brooks and invites me to his office, closing the door behind us.

"Your complaint regarding Michael Hawkins has come to my attention," he says, gesturing with his hand toward the chairs in front of his desk.

I nod and sit, waiting for him to continue. My anger has vanished completely and is replaced with anxiety at the sight of the judging look on Lieutenant Brooks' face.

He places the document on his desk and sits back on his chair, clasping his hands on the desk. "You stated that a video of you was recorded while having sex with Zane Hawkins, Michael Hawkins' son." He looks up at me and I nod.

"That's right."

"And, you work as an escort to Michael Hawkins."

"That's... No, that's not correct. Michael Hawkins hired me as a data analyst in the marketing department of Hawkins Media."

"Here you say *'I'm contracted by Michael Hawkins to attend special events as his companion for a period of one year. He threatened to upload the contents of the contract together with the video recording online if I don't follow his orders, including but not limited to having sex with his clients.'* Miss Garnett, you must know prostitution is illegal in California. You can get serious jail time." His voice is calm but menacing, and I can't help but feel I'm the criminal here rather than the victim.

"I can assure you, sir, I'm not working as a prostitute. I only agreed to go on dates to special events with Michael Hawkins as a favor."

"But here it says you signed a contract."

"Yes, but it was mainly for confidentiality reasons. I never agreed on anything sexual. Not even a kiss."

"Do you have the contract or a copy of it with you?"

"I do. A scanned copy in my phone."

He nods, giving me permission to get my phone. I fish it out of my bag, my hands trembling while I skim through the folders. "Here it is." I place the phone on his desk so he can get it.

He gazes at the screen of my phone with the utmost focus, and I can't help but worry how some conditions stated in the contract can be misinterpreted.

"Would you mind if I print it out?"

"No, go ahead." I watch him anxiously as he hooks up my phone to his computer with an uncomfortable feeling of fear falling over me. I'm really doing this, violating the main condition of the contract: The confidentiality of Michael's sexual orientation, giving him the right to sue me. I don't have any tangible proof of his blackmail; neither a voice recording of his words nor the sex tape itself. It'll be my word against his.

"Did anyone witness your and Mr. Hawkins's conversation during the incident?"

I shake my head no.

"Can you provide any evidence or proof of harassment?"

"No."

As the minutes pass, I'm getting less confident about my complaint. I may get lucky if there've been other complaints against him, but otherwise, Lieutenant Brooks' questions give me the impression that my complaint will not help, just put me in trouble for violating the main rule of the contract.

I hear the printer and watch as the papers slide out of the machine. Lieutenant Brooks hands me my phone and gets up to gather the printouts. "I'll have an officer look into your case. However, I can't promise the investigation will lead to anywhere without any concrete evidence."

My head drops with disappointment. How can I get evidence to support my complaint? I can get Zane to testify, but I doubt he will be willing for the same reasons of confidentiality as an employee at Hawkins Media Group. The easiest way would be to go back to Michael's office with a voice recorder and have him repeat his threats. Pushing his button so he pours out all his anger to me shouldn't be a big deal, considering how easily he showed me his real face right after I'd declined to join his weekend party. I will repeat the same lines, claiming to have other plans, and just watch him repeat the threats as the recorder captures his words.

The Trap

Lieutenant Brooks asks me to wait while he enters my case into the database. I comply, although I'm not sure why he has to do it again after the female officer did it already. After nearly half an hour of watching him type, I get impatient, mostly because I don't want to waste an extra minute, garnering proof on my case.

As soon as Lieutenant Brooks makes me sign

some documents regarding my complaint, I get to my feet with renewed confidence and thank him for his help, even though he didn't at all.

Clutching my purse with both hands, I head toward the exit but come to a sudden halt when Ace appears at the security screening. He looks miserable while a police officer scans his body with a metal detector. Once he's through, he paces toward me and grabs me by the elbow to pull me aside.

"Have you filed a complaint already?" His voice is low as he speaks.

I nod, apprehensive at the agony on his face. "How do you know about the complaint?" Did he talk to Zane? Although I'm not sure how Zane knew about my intentions to go to police, let alone to which police station specifically. It might not be Zane, though. Michael must have sent someone to follow my every step. For all I know, Michael attached a GPS device to my Audi to track my whereabouts. I think I should go back to driving my old coupe, however, I'm afraid it won't be immune to Michael's manipulations either.

"I'll tell you in the car," Ace says. "But before we leave, you should withdraw your complaint."

"What? No way."

"Please, if you don't do it, he'll hurt Chloe." He lowers his head to whisper in my ear, but the second before his face gets lost in my hair, I note fear spreading on his beautiful features. "Last night, he beat her up. She was in terrible pain when I saw her, so I took her to a friend of mine to hide her from him. But when I phoned them today, they didn't answer my calls. Then Michael called me to tell me that he has Chloe and won't release her if I don't stop you from filing a complaint against him."

"Goddammit, are you sure?" Michael might be a monster, but fuck it, Chloe is his own daughter.

Ace moves away from me, nodding, and produces a mobile phone from his pocket. I stare down at the screen with shock forcing my mouth to pop open at the picture of Chloe taped and bruised. Her eyes are closed, perhaps because she's sleeping. Hopefully not because she blacked out. Oh, God. He wasn't lying. Michael is more dangerous than I thought. If he can do this to his own child, I can't even begin to imagine what he has in store for me.

Ace runs his hands through his hair, letting

out a breath of hopelessness, anger, and shock. Everything I feel right now.

What kind of beast have I crossed ways with? A monster who pushed his wife to suicide while torturing his children and abusing total strangers purely for his own benefit?

Macey Williams has the excuse of growing up in poverty without a father and most likely numerous mental issues. What's Michael's excuse to spread malice? It's not like having to repress one's sexual preferences causes one to commit a crime. Was it his parents who robbed him of his feeling of empathy by abusing him, or is it some chemical imbalance in his brain that's causing his irrational and cruel deeds?

Whatever the trigger is, I have a nagging feeling that if it wasn't Chloe, it'd be someone else. Maybe Taylor. She already suffered enough for half a dozen lifetimes; she doesn't need any more traumas to break her down completely.

I don't have any real attachment to Chloe, but she's an innocent in the hands of a criminal, and if her wellbeing depends on my withdrawal of my complaint, so be it. I can't live with the fact that someone else is being tormented for my actions. "Okay, I'll do it."

An uncomfortable feeling of guilt takes over me as I walk back to the female officer who initially took my case. This is how lawbreakers get away with their crimes. By coercing their victims with blackmail. I may be taking a step back with my action now, but I swear I'll make Michael pay for everything. I don't know how exactly I will do that, but I won't stop even if it takes my entire lifetime. I'll make him regret this.

The female officer listens to me as I explain how I misunderstood Michael's words and twisted them into malice, as if I'm the dumbest person in a hundred-mile radius, and watch her while she looks up my file on the computer. Her bored and disinterested expression makes me feel relieved. I wouldn't be the first one to pull a complaint. At least my real motivation, not the one I told the officer, is for the sake of someone's wellbeing.

The officer makes me sign a document and calls the next person in line. I stroll toward the exit beside Ace and follow him out to the street.

"Someone from the inside leaked out the information about your complaint," Ace whispers to me, his eyes scanning the people passing by.

Oh my God. Michael had that much reach? He has people working for him in the police department too? I don't even know why I am surprised. That's the only way he can continue his crimes and not get caught red handed.

"I'll call him and tell him I'm ready to do anything he wants so he lets Chloe go." The thought of being the reason for someone else's suffering is making me sick. I'd rather go through that pain myself.

Without waiting for a reaction from Ace, I grab my phone inside my purse and dial Michael's cell. One beep turns to two, three, six, ten, but no one picks up. Not even his voice mail. Michael must already know he has me completely under his control, that's why he doesn't accept my call. I swallow the feeling of defeat and drop my cell back into my purse. "What are we going to do now? Do you know what exactly happened to Chloe?"

We walk to the parking lot where my car is parked and get inside. I grab my car keys but don't turn on the engine, waiting for Ace to explain the details.

"Michael beat her up last night. She was going to fly to Guatemala today, but I arranged a place for her to stay with a friend of mine. Michael must have known my plans or had me followed, I don't know, but today when I called my friend to ask how Chloe was doing, she didn't answer her phone. I drove up to her home but couldn't find her or Chloe there. The door to her apartment was open and the inside looked like a robbery had taken place. Then, I received the picture I showed you. Michael kidnapped both Chloe and Diana."

"What the fuck! What's wrong with him? Seriously, I don't understand it." Why am I asking Ace that? He must have seen Michael at his worst and still couldn't figure out the why's and how's. No one with a sound mind can.

"What did you talk with Michael about? What did you want to file a complaint about?"

I let out a loud breath and look out through the windshield. How will I tell him about the sex tape with Zane without feeling embarrassed? Particularly only a couple of hours after opening up to him at the deepest, most primal level. With my body and soul.

"He ordered me to join him for the next weekend while he's hosting some important guests and threatened to put a sex tape of Zane and me online if I didn't obey him."

"Sex tape of you and ...?" He can't finish his sentence. I feel so dirty right now. I wish the earth would swallow me whole at this moment rather than having to see the disappointment in Ace's eyes.

"It was during the day of the coconut-oil incident. Turns out it was all Zane's plan," I say to divert his attention to something else and see the flames of anger flaring up on his face. He starts to open his mouth but I raise my hand to stop him. "He was planning to put it on the internet so everyone could see Michael and I didn't share any romantic interest toward each other. Michael and I would have to end our fake romance if Zane's plan worked out. That was going to be Zane's way of releasing me from Michael. He swears he didn't have any other intentions for recording the video besides that."

"You're making a mistake by trusting him. He never plays by the rules of a fair game. He and Michael must be in this together, and Zane's explanation might be a way to gain your trust so they know your next step and continue holding you under control."

I drop my gaze at my hands in my lap in confusion. Ace might be right, but my instincts are telling me to give Zane a chance. Only, I don't know if I can trust my instincts anymore. They were right about the contract I signed with Michael, yet totally wrong about Michael's personality. Maybe I should ignore my feelings and concentrate on facts only. Even if I have no way to figure out Zane's real intentions, I can test him and even take advantage of his motivation to gain my trust.

"What happened with Michael?" Ace distracts my thoughts.

"He threatened to put the video online together with the contract to show everyone what a cheap whore I was to work as an escort for him and serve his son. Also he said he'd ruin my sister's company by canceling the project he has with her."

"You came to the police to file a complaint about him despite all those threats?" There's a surprising hint of admiration in his voice, which is the only thing that lifts up my spirits in this mess called my Sunday afternoon.

"Zane talked me into it," I admit and convey everything Zane told me about the confidentiality of the contract and how Michael would risk being sued by leaking the contract to the public, and my conversation with the officer.

Ace shifts in his seat and shakes his head.

"Still, be very wary of his promises." I can see the protective string in his personality being pulled to the highest. His sister is in danger, and as if that's not enough, he's worrying about me as well.

"What are we going to do about Chloe? I can't believe Michael will hurt her."

"This isn't the first time he's hurt her. She's seen his evil side more than anyone else. Michael was aggressive to Zane and me, but it was nothing in comparison to how Chloe suffered through his anger attacks. I don't know what he has against her, but he can't seem to stop hurting her to the point of breaking her. Even so, this is new. Kidnapping Chloe and using her to control someone else is unheard of for Michael. I always thought he must have some twisted, overly protective fatherly instinct in him that pushes him out of control when it came to Chloe. But this last act proved me wrong."

"We have to find a way to save her before..." The words are too painful to spell out, even to think of. Having seen a glimpse of Michael's evil side, thinking about the magnitude of damage he can inflict upon Chloe turns my stomach upside down.

Ace inhales deeply, his chin shaking as his

chest widens with the breath. "I'll make him pay for it. Even if it's the last thing I do on earth, I'll put an end to his insolence."

"I'm with you in this. We'll save her together. I don't know how, but we will."

He gives me a nod of acceptance, his features softening visibly with relief.

I reach for his fist and cover it with my hand. I feel I can trust him without hesitation. He won't turn his back on me or leave me hanging when he saves Chloe; he is there for me too. To protect me from Michael's wickedness. "We need a plan," I say with desperation throbbing inside my chest at the sight of Ace's pained look. "First we need to find out what he really wants from me, the real reason why he hired me in the first place."

He lifts his free hand and reaches for my lips to silence me. Perhaps he anticipates what I'm about to say. That it is all my fault. Chloe's kidnapping. Michael's extra pressure on Ace. Even the frustration Ace has over the sex tape of me with Zane, however insignificant it might be, considering Chloe's kidnapping.

If I hadn't signed that contract with Michael ...

As if hearing my thoughts and not wanting me to draw a conclusion out of them, he sneaks his hand around my neck and draws me against him for a kiss that's worthy enough to forget about Michael and his evil plans about Chloe and me.

Ace draws in a deep breath of air as if it's me he's inhaling instead of air. His lips move softly yet demanding around mine as are his hands on my arms and shoulders. He's everything my body yearns for. I can't believe how I managed to survive without him before.

Tears sting my eyes at the possibility of seeing Ace hurt. I might be in danger but watching pain pour out of his skin hurts me as if he's a part of my body.

What if Michael really does something horrible to Chloe? Worse than what he has done, that is. Will I be able to live with the fact that I'm the reason why everything started in the first place? Even if I did, will Ace ever be able to overlook that fact?

My fingers clutch around his collar in an attempt to plaster his lips harder against mine. I've just discovered he's the one I've been searching for all my life, how can I stay sane if I lose him?

Our kiss deepens despite my sobs. I'm crying and letting him love me. It's like our tangled lips are filling us up with hope and belief that we can do this together. As if we're signing a secret contract about our partnership in this hardship. Our lips seal the deal. Even without our signatures, this agreement is harder to break than any other contract I've signed, including Michael's.

Ace pulls back, and I can only admire his beautiful, sky-blue eyes, wet like mine. Books should be written about the depths of his irises, thickness of the lush, blond lashes, and the unspoken words they inflict into my heart.

Zane was right. Not everything is entirely bad. Even the most evil thing has something good in it, like Ace showing up in my life after that goddamn contract I signed with Michael. I'd never have gotten to know this man, who knows my body better than me and has already started staking his claim on my heart, if it wasn't for Michael's ulterior motive to hire me.

"Let's go home," Ace says, catching me by surprise. *Home?* As if it's something we both own and share together. I don't correct him or ask for clarification. I just nod and insert the key to the ignition. Michael forbade me any kind of relationship with Ace, but I guess if he can change the rules of the game he started, then so can I with Ace's help.

The Realization - ACE

I knew Michael would pull off something cruel to gain the upper hand. I saw it coming. But never in a million years would I have imagined him using Chloe to get what he wanted. That new information erases the minuscule reasoning I had in my mind about his over-protectiveness as the motivation behind his cruelties.

Lindsay too surprised me today. I somehow

guessed she'd back down from her complaint, but I wasn't counting on her siding with me to rescue Chloe and her instant faith in our ability to defeat Michael despite the odds against us, like she's not aware of the magnitude of his power. Isn't that the kind of person who actually beats the unbeatable, demolishes the rules, and starts a revolution?

God, she even intended to file a complaint against Michael. I'm sure as hell no one, even the politicians themselves, have dared to even consider that possibility. She's brave to the level of crazy, but I'd rather have her crazy with braveness than indifferent to my sister's suffering. As long as her craziness doesn't get her in trouble. To ensure that, I'll have to keep her around, though it'll most likely attract more of Michael's anger.

Where can Chloe be right now? What's she doing? I put Diana in danger as well by asking for her help. I should have seen my plan wasn't a great one. Michael has eyes everywhere. He must have known about Chloe's absence since the minute she ran away to Diana's home.

Lindsay snuggles up against me on the couch in my living room, pulling my head down against her chest, distracting my troublesome thoughts. I'm thankful for having her as my distraction or else I'd have no idea about how to pass a second knowing Chloe is in danger and not being able to help her.

Lindsay's heartbeats are loud and fast, so must be the fear running rampant in her head. I should have the same conviction as her and believe we have a chance to turn the tables against Michael, however small that chance might be.

My arms are loosely around her waist, her hands holding my shoulders. Her body feels like an extension of mine, so natural, even necessary, and makes me marvel about the false feeling of security I'd shrouded myself in before she came into my life. Having Lindsay's body around mine, like a shield guarding me, provides me with a more tangible sense of safety than I've ever felt in my life, despite the severity of the circumstances surrounding us. While it should have been me as a man doing so she has generously taken over that duty.

"We need a plan," she whispers, her breath against my hair. I wish I could prolong the silence and peace I have while in her arms, but she won't calm down and let go without sharpening her knives ready for a bloody fight. "For that, we need to find out why Michael wanted to hire me in the first place. I have no doubt he wants more than just to have me as his fake girlfriend. He's after something big, I can feel it. That's why he's using Chloe, but I have no fucking idea what he could want from me. If I knew it, I'd give it to him right away. Nothing is more important than your sister's life."

Her words pinch at my heart. She's right. If Michael is playing dangerous, that means he's after something big. Perhaps he won't kill Chloe — he's not that much of a monster, I hope— but every minute she's in his hands must be traumatizing for her. And I don't have the slightest idea what he'll do to my friend, Diana.

"Do you have any idea what he might want from me?" Lindsay asks, tilting her head up to meet my gaze.

I straighten up and shake my head no. "No idea."

"I thought you'd say that. Well, let's brainstorm about the options. I'm a relatively famous woman thanks to the video where I killed someone. I'm also a mathematician with only one year of experience, an orphan, the sister of a successful businesswoman, and have a history of a sexual harassment lawsuit. Any of that jog your brain?"

I can't help smiling. I wasn't wrong in my first impression that she has an interesting persona. "I have to admit, I don't know much about how or why you killed that woman."

"Macey Williams was the half-sister of my sister's ex-husband, Jack. After Jack died, he left Taylor an inheritance of several million dollars." She looks up at the ceiling, drawing her eyebrows together, while she's thinking. "More than a hundred million dollars actually. Macey tried to get rid of my sister to get her hands on the money and kidnapped me to lure Taylor in. Taylor was pregnant at that time." Her voice falters and I notice a tear slipping down her cheek.

"Let's do it later if it's hard for you to talk about it."

"No, I'm fine. It's just ... it was very hard for us all because Taylor's baby had a birth defect. She'd been trying to get pregnant for so long, then came the birth defect."

"I'm sorry, baby."

"Anyway, Taylor wasn't in good condition health-wise, and when Macey kidnapped us, Taylor went into labor. I thought she'd die with the heavy blood loss, and I lost my sanity for a few seconds. I don't remember much about how I killed her exactly, but I remember being filled with rage seeing my sister so close to death."

Fear overtakes me with the thought of Lindsay being face to face with a maniac. The circumstances she had with Macey Williams haven't changed much. Michael is as insane as Macey was, only with more money and better-calculated plans.

"I just slapped her with all the anger boiling inside me," she continues. "I didn't think what would happen to her. I just wanted to stop her before she could hurt my sister, but I ended up stopping her for good." More tears follow and her pink skin glows with moistness.

I slip my thumbs across her cheeks to dry them. "You're dangerous when you're angry, you know that?"

She snorts and shakes her head. "Don't get started with how scary I am again."

That's not a bad thing to be, but I keep that thought to myself. "Tell me more about your sister. Did she start the construction company?"

"No, not at all. She didn't have the slightest

idea about the construction business. She inherited the company from her deceased husband. Adam, her current husband, helped her a lot in the beginning. It was a relatively small company until they took over Michael's residential project. Apparently, it's the biggest project they have ever had and it brought a lot of attention to Taylor's company and helped them get more projects from other clients."

"Do you know anything about the project?" I ask.

"I was gonna ask you that. You don't?"

"No, not at all. Michael doesn't share anything regarding his business with me."

"Well, you know the property used to belong to Chloe's boyfriend's family."

I nod and she continues. "I think it was a great idea to turn the country club to a more useful area with residential buildings, single homes, and town houses. Half of the territory is already planted with trees too, or so I hear. So in theory, it's a great project because Michael will make lots of money and for people looking for a good location to buy homes close to LA. I mean country clubs are just a waste of land. Don't you think?"

"Sure. Is the construction going well?"

"Of course it is. My sister and her husband are a great team. So, does anything sound suspicious to you? Can Michael be after me for something related to the construction project?"

I shrug. "I can't think of a reason why. If he wants something specific, he can simply order them to do it. He doesn't need to go after you; after all, he has the money and the complete control over the project. How about the company you worked for in New York? Was it a governmental agency?"

"No, not even close. It was a cosmetics company, and I worked in the marketing department."

"Did you work in the same department with the man who tried to ..." Fuck! I can't keep my hands from forming fists at the thought of a man coming close to forcing Lindsay into sex. If I had that motherfucker in front of me right now, I'd make sure he couldn't use his dick anymore, even for urinating.

"Yes, he was the director of the marketing department."

"How did it happen?" Not that it's relevant to

our case with Michael, but I have to know the details even though it'll make me angrier than anything else ever has.

"You don't wanna hear that." She moves close to me, bringing her face only an inch away from mine. Her stare is full of provocation and also pleas. I see the hurt and fear deep down in her eyes that glow like onyx with the tears still moistening them. What has she gone through? There's so much I don't know about her.

"No, I don't but I have to. I want to know your deepest secrets, Lindsay, even if some of them are wounding."

"His name is Don Sheridan. He was very kind, very helpful, during my first months at the company. Everyone in the department loved him and praised him for being a great boss. He was also a family man—father, married with four kids. I didn't think much about his friendliness at first. I just thought he was doing his job by showing me extra attention as a beginner on the team. I even met his wife and kids during a Christmas party he hosted at his home." She pauses to make sure I want to hear the rest and continues as soon as I nod my encouragement. "Then, his closeness took new heights. He wanted to go to lunch with me, take me to conferences in other cities. Started asking about my private life, if I was dating anyone, if I wanted to marry my then boyfriend, saying things like I was too young to take any relationship seriously, I should enjoy my youth and beauty and be with as many men as possible ... and more bullshit like that."

I swallow, working hard not to show my anger, but it's fucking impossible while picturing Lindsay defenseless against a man.

"The incident happened during one of the conferences. He walked me to my room in the hotel where we were staying, and when I unlocked the door and told him goodbye, he covered my mouth and pushed me inside ..."

"All right. Enough." I can't take hearing more details. My hands start shaking, and my breath becomes shallow and heavy. "Take your jeans off," I order.

Her eyes widen with shock and maybe dismay. "Does that arouse you? My fucking rape story turned you on, didn't it?"

"No, fuck. I can't bear the thought of a man being so close to you. Now do what I say."

She smirks and throws herself back at the

sofa across from me, and of course doesn't do what I asked her to do. I sneak my hand between her legs to cup her crotch. She flinches at my rough touch but doesn't push my hand away. I rub it roughly with my palm first and push my thumb against her entrance through the jeans. She gazes at me with curious eyes that are hooded with her heavy eyelids and moans softly.

"I can't share you with another man." With my other hand, I unbutton and unzip her jeans. Her hips move back and forth against my hand, and I imagine the warm wetness that is awaiting me behind the fabric of her jeans.

"You watched me having sex with ..."

"Stop," I yell. I've been trying to erase the memory of JJ having her in front of me from my mind. Without any success obviously, because now her moans while JJ was inside her fill my head again. Fuck it.

Pulling down her jeans, I yank them away. My sister is kidnapped. Michael is likely hatching a series of vicious plans to destroy me and the people I love, but all I can think of, all my mind can register right now is the acute desire to watch Lindsay startle as I explore the swollen lips of her sex with my fingers. Hear her moan as I force myself inside her. Feel her love as I make her mine again. "Did you want your boss to approach you?"

"No." Her eyes grow wide with anger in an instant and she glues her knees together.

Her denial of access to me infuriates my own rage. "Did you find him attractive?"

"No."

"Did you want to fuck him?"

"Cut it out. I didn't want to do anything with him. I don't fuck married men." Her voice shakes, and I won't be surprised if she tries to punch me in the face for my insult. My heart pinches at the hurt expression playing on her face, yet I can't find it in me to cool down.

Slipping a hand between her thighs, I force my way down to her panties and move over to her. She tightens her thighs to stop me, but I reach down and grab the inside of her panties, feeling her soft, moist flesh with the tip of my fingers. "You won't fuck another man, single or married," I hiss. "You're mine now."

I never had a possessive streak in me for a girl in my life. I wouldn't flinch a finger if one of the women I had sex with slept with another man in front of my eyes, but the possibility of Lindsay being intimate with someone else is enough to make my blood boil.

"You're mine," I repeat, this time with a softer, less hostile tone. She's breathing heavily, most likely calculating how best to kick me in the crotch or give me a taste of her iron slap to show me my place. She wouldn't be completely wrong for choosing violence against my hostility. Who claims ownership of a girl after merely two days of what, just sex? However, nothing comes; no hitting, no opposition.

I slip my index finger through her swollen folds, then inside her channel to probe a reaction out of her. She must be shocked at my outrage, that's all. Once it wears off, she'll show me. The idea of getting her heated up thrills me even more, add to that the tight wrap of her insides around my finger, and I'm seconds away from launching myself onto her petite body. My cock springs up to life, pushing against my own jeans as my finger goes deeper and deeper.

"Aghrrr." She closes her eyes shut and drops her head against the arm of the couch. I come an inch away from crushing my lips down to hers when she murmurs, "Okay," in the middle of her moan.

I'm an idiot for asking her for clarification, but I do it anyway. "Okay what?" I bend my index finger like a hook and slowly slip it out of her, its tip grating against the heated flesh of her sex.

Her body arches up with my drawn-out insult, and she spreads her legs open. "I'm ... oh God. I'm yours."

It takes very little strength to rip off her panties and a short time to get rid of my jeans and boxers, and soon, I'm positioned between her thighs, our hips against each other, her sex opening up to me with a welcoming heat. My entire body throbs with the need to feel her insides. I want to get lost in the fire of lust her body is radiating and leave everything else into nothingness.

She's giving out soft moans as I slide into her to the hilt. Her hands are grabbing my arms as a warning to take it slowly, as if it's her first time. I ride her with gentle strokes, trying to grasp the novelty of having sex with a girl who I just declared to be mine and to sort out the wild emotions that are making my heart beat fast and furious inside my chest. To figure out if this is the right way to go. She's a target for Michael. My unusual interest in her will upset him more than anything. He'll attempt to ruin her too, as always he did to everything and everyone I cared about.

Her legs move up and lock around my hips, and I let my body fall on her, squeezing her fragile torso against the couch. Her cheeks are glowing red. Her eyes are following me with intent but close each time I drive into her.

With each new thrust, I'm engulfed by newfound confidence and assurance that I can stand up to Michael, although this is the cruelest I've ever seen him be. It's as if Lindsay is transferring her inner strength into me, turning me into the man I should have been years ago, rather than the coward I've been all this time, the one who always shut his eyes against Michael's viciousness.

It's true what they say. A man's true strength comes from the woman behind him. Only, Lindsay doesn't just stand behind me, she's beside me, and I have no doubt she will fight to get in front of me at the first opportunity.

I lean down and lick her lips, parting them apart. She accepts my tongue in and sucks it ferociously. My hands work the buttons of her shirt until I reach her bra. Pulling it down, I start rubbing her erect nipples. She pushes her body against my hands with need. Her sex squeezes my cock close to a hard release.

She's perfect for me, the sensual contours and crevices of her petite figure, the silky smoothness of her skin, the responsiveness of her body. The constant dare in her fierce eyes, the sweet softness of her lips.

She's been the faceless woman in my erotic fantasies. But what makes her the ideal woman for me is her entire being—her outspokenness, fearlessness, and her readiness to make sacrifices to protect her loved ones. That's why my fall for her was quick like lightening, and I'll be damned if I let her go or out of sight even for a day. I don't have any control over her interaction with other men in the past, although it pains me to think of the two men that touched her are from my business. But, I'll do anything to keep her interest in only me and protect her from Michael's associates.

Anything.

I couldn't be there for my mother. I couldn't stand up for Chloe. But I'll not let anyone hurt Lindsay, and this'll be the greatest test of my life. If I fail it, I don't have a reason to live.

The Ex

I don't know where all this is coming from. I've never been claimed by someone, much less after only a couple weeks of having met. Ace, however, not only just declared himself as my owner, but also convinced me with mere words that it's indeed the truth.

The way he touches me, careful like I'm an exquisite piece of china worth millions of dollars, yet his kisses selfish and ruthless like I'm a sex doll made only for his enjoyment, heat up my blood and loosen my resolve. If anyone should be allowed to use me that way, it's Ace, because seeing him orgasm inside me and with me is a sight worth life itself.

His hands roam all over my body, rubbing my sensitive skin close to the pinnacle. What we're doing is insane. Mating, while danger is only a few steps away? While someone's life is in grave danger? But I let him be as rough with me as he wants. He needs this, and I'd be lying if I said the urgency to be with him isn't getting under my skin and pushing me to madness.

I close my eyes, feeling his hot breath on my skin, trying hard to memorize each second, engrave the thrill running wild through my body into my mind, so I won't forget how beautiful sex actually is when the most difficult of times comes if—most likely, when— Michael offers me to his guests as a sex slave.

I want to cry my eyes out for the happiness pouring out of me with each forceful kiss from Ace and the possessive touch of his hands as if he won't let anyone hurt me. But I know there're things we can't avoid no matter what we do.

What will become of me afterward? Will I be

able to feel the same sweet sensations again? Or will I hate men and everything related to them? I don't have the slightest idea how sadistic men can be, or if I'll be able to keep a piece of myself despite the horror, but at least I have something to hold on to, someone to be there for me.

I hug him and kiss him, letting my body go loose as the climax hits me wild and strong and rolls through my body like a violent storm. This very second where I can see through the eyes of my soul, feeling the breathtaking beauty of uniting with someone as special as Ace should be my reference point when everything starts crushing down on me. I should remember this once-in-a-lifetime encounter of two lost souls finding each other in the midst of filth and terror.

There must be a reason why I entered Ace's life and he mine. Why I find myself in the middle of the dirtiest of intrigues ... Why he has such a strong, undeniable pull on me ... I can feel it in the deepest, darkest part of my heart that it is to put an end to Michael's cruelties: his maltreatment of Chloe, Ace, even Zane.

Determination throbs inside me, filling me up to the brim. I'll find a way to defeat Michael. And I'll be damned if the key to his destruction doesn't lie in the hidden reason for my recruitment as his girlfriend.

I hold my gaze on Ace's beautiful face while he finds his release, pushing me to the edge of the couch with its force. His expression is tender and heartwarming. I reach up and run the tip of my fingers across his lips. His mouth opens but heavy breaths stop him from speaking.

I wish I had access to his thoughts to see if he's feeling the same as I am. If his heart too is spreading and constricting with affection and marvel. If the very thought of me getting hurt is painful enough to paralyze him because I feel the same way about him ... If he too is astounded by the inconceivable level of pleasure our intimacy is emitting ...

And if this all is new to him too.

We lie down on the couch facing each other, neither of us having the courage to talk, not wanting to ruin the beauty of the moment. He closes his eyes and I feel the weight of his arm around my hip getting heavier as he drifts into sleep. I'm too alert to even consider dozing off at this moment.

Slipping out of his hold, I reach for my

clothes and put them on. If I don't do something about Chloe's situation now, I'll probably lose my mind, and no amount of sex with Ace can save me from that.

I find my phone in my purse and step out to the balcony, closing its door so as not to disturb Ace. The darkness soothes my agitated nerves. The chilly weather cools down my over-heated head. The digital clock on my phone reads 7:50 PM. What a day it has been, filled with delightfulness at getting to know Ace, to the bombshell of seeing Michael's true colors.

What I need now more than anything is information, and the only person who can provide me with it is Zane. I dial his number, stealing a glance at Ace to make sure he's still sleeping.

"Hey, there," Zane greets me with an oddly cheerful tone, considering the circumstances. Likely because he doesn't know about Chloe's kidnapping.

"Hello. I take it that you haven't heard Chloe's missing."

"Who is missing?" His voice turns cold and angry in an instant.

I explain to him about my attempt to file a

complaint against Michael, and Chloe's kidnapping, and listen to the curses rolling out of Zane's mouth one after another. "We need to save Chloe, and we can do it if we can find out what Michael wants from me. Do you have any idea why he hired me?"

"I'm as clueless about his plans as you are, honey. I tried to get his secretary, Julie, to talk, but she doesn't know anything about the reason for your recruitment either." The way he says his last sentence makes me wonder about the method he used to get Julie to talk, but it's most likely the same method he used on me to record a sex video of us. His charm knows no bounds, I guess, or at least that's what he thinks, if he tried it on someone like Julie, who has access to practically everything business-related about Michael. If Zane is right and Julie doesn't know anything, does that mean Michael's special interest in me is more on the personal level?

"Edrick should know something. Can you get him to talk?" I ask.

"Yeah, he might, but I guess you have a better chance to get information out of him than I do. He hates me to the core." I suppose his charm does indeed have limits.

"Why? Did you sleep with his sister?" I joke.

"No, not his sister, his mother."

"Ewww."

His revelation makes me feel dirty for having slept with him, more so for having Ace in my life now. How stupid of me it was to let Zane play with me in my apartment. Where was my oh-so-smart brain? However, Zane's dirty appetite for women might have its perks as well. "Good for you. Are you in contact with any of Michael's ex's? They might have noticed something that could be relevant to our problem."

"Funny you say that. I'm actually planning to meet the one before you tonight. Tiffany Jordan."

"Her name rings a bell. Is she famous?"

"Famous? Only this year's Oscar award winner for best actress. Anyway, I'm going out to dinner with her. Hey, hold on a sec ... I've just gotten a memo from Julie. Looks like Michael left for New York and won't be back until the weekend."

Oh, the fucking weekend. I hope his plane blows up in the air so he won't make it back. "Can you arrange a meeting for me with Tiffany Jordan?"

"Come and join us for dinner. I never say no to a threesome offer."

"You fucking bastard. Your sister is in danger. How can you behave like it's a normal day?"

"I'm fucked up, I know. But my offer is still on. I'll text you the address of the restaurant if you want to meet with her."

"Okay, do that." I disconnect and wait for his text. When my phone beeps with an incoming message, I notice from the corner of my eye that Ace shifts on the couch. I turn around to see him looking around in horror then relax as soon as he locates me. He must be worried about me too, in addition to his sister, and I can't help but feel gratitude for having him by my side, even if he's as helpless as I am.

After reading the text from Zane, I open the balcony door and enter the living room, letting Ace's loving gaze and completely naked body heat up my blood.

"I'll leave in a few." I scoot next to him and grab his arm to wrap it around my shoulder. If I had any chill left in my body, it disappears in an instant with the heat radiating from his large, firm body. I lock my arms around his hips and rub my chest against the side of his torso.

He gives me a sexy smile and drops his head to leave a kiss on my nose. "Stay tonight."

"Okay," I say way too easily. "But I have to meet with someone. It won't last long, an hour or two, tops."

"Who?" His blond eyebrows push together in the most adoring way, and I can't help but smile at his curiosity mixed with jealousy.

"Michael's ex. Tiffany Jordan. I think she might be able to give me some information that could be useful."

Scowling, he reaches to tuck a lock of hair behind my ear and then runs the back of his hand on my cheek. The hair on my neck stands at the soft touch of his fingers, and I forget instantly what I was about to say, or if I was going to say anything at all.

"How did you set it up so fast? Do you know her?"

I shake my head. "I don't, but Zane does, and from the sound of it, he *knows* her quite well."

"Zane?" His scowl deepens. "Were you just

talking to him?"

"Yeah. I thought he ..." I swallow hard at the sight of anger twisting his expression, making him look lethal. "What's going on?"

"You're making a huge mistake by trusting him. I have no doubt he's siding with Michael in this. He's pretending to be on your side only to find out your next step. As soon as he knows what you're up to, Michael will know it too."

"You might be right, but what else can I do?" He doesn't reply, so I continue. "Besides, it's not too bad if he thinks I trust him. It'll give us a chance to fool him easily if we need to someday."

"I like the way you think, but be very careful around him," he says matter-of-factly as if to say *'Don't fall for his charm and let him fuck you again.'* I feel my cheeks heat up with embarrassment. "And I'm coming with you," he adds, saving me from my shame. Seriously, what came over me that I allowed Zane to take me?

"He might get upset," I point out.

"He can get upset all he wants. You shouldn't be alone at this point. We don't know what Michael has in mind. He might try to kidnap you as well."

A shiver of fear courses through my body. As much as I fear for Chloe's wellbeing, I dread the thought of me at Michael's mercy. If Michael kidnaps me, I'll end up in a much worse situation than Chloe. After all, she's his daughter, and I'm practically nobody to him.

"If Michael wanted to kidnap me, nobody could stop him." I find myself stating the ugly truth. That he didn't kidnap me and lets me free for the moment means something.

He lets out a deep breath of frustration, his eyes blazing with desperation and helplessness. I should be kinder with him and keep my blatant side in check, especially in a delicate situation like this one. "Yes, come with me. I'll feel safer with you." I place my head on his shoulder and plaster my lips against his skin.

Would I feel this close to Ace if it weren't for Michael's viciousness? Most likely not. Who would have thought I'd have something to thank Michael for?

We get ready quickly and drive to the restaurant with Ace's car. He holds my hand as we enter the restaurant and ask the hostess for Zane's table. I doubt something will come out of this meeting, but still it might give us a hint related to

Michael's plans.

A young, blonde waitress walks us to a secluded part of the restaurant, and I scan around anxiously. Perhaps Michael sent one of his men to have me followed, and now he'll know I'm meeting with one of his exes.

Would that put Tiffany Jordan in danger? Oh God, no. What if Michael decides to punish her too, if she gives away sensitive information? Maybe this wasn't a good idea, but now it's too late to turn around and leave because Michael must have already found out my plans and decided to add Tiffany to his list of people he will harass.

I spot Zane and a tall, brunette woman beside him. She must be at least thirty, but her beauty could hold its own against anyone younger. I see her lips flicker up in a scorning smile as she stands and holds out her hand for me.

"You must be Lindsay Doheny." Her handshake is firm, a little too tight for a friendly meeting. Her eyes do a quick once-over on my body, and her smile widens, perhaps acknowledging that I'm not as pretty as she is. "Ace." She turns once she's done evaluating my looks and steps toward Ace. "Long time no see. How are you? You look as good as I remember."

Only then do I see the murderous look on Zane's face directed at Ace. He doesn't bother to stand but pulls a chair beside him for me to sit. Ace keeps my hand laced in his while shaking hands with Tiffany. Tiffany stands a little too close to Ace and bites her lower lip as she runs a hand along Ace's arm. What a bitch! Isn't she here on a date with Zane? Why is she acting as if Ace is the one she'll end up in bed with?

Wait a minute.

I look up at Ace and then at Tiffany to get a hint of the reason for the unusual charge of electricity in the air. Did he fuck her too? I narrow my eyes at Tiffany with hatred, but I'm guilty of the same crime for having been intimate with both Ace and Zane. I don't know if I should be happy or upset about not being the first girl who had both men.

I pull Ace's hand to end Tiffany's discomfortingly close proximity to Ace, and he gets my message and settles on the chair between Tiffany and me.

"So, Ace," Zane says, giving dirty looks to him. "How are you doing other than screwing the women I slept with? So typical of you. Are you planning to change that habit, ever?"

"Oh, shut up," I hiss between my teeth before Ace can pour out his anger. For now, he should be content with squeezing my hand tight, which I can't say I'll be able to handle for long, because my bones start throbbing with pain. I shake his hand to make him aware of my pain, and he softens his hold instantly. But I suppose I won't be able to do anything about the scary iciness of his face. "We didn't come here to fight. Your sister is in danger for God's sake. Keep your claws in check and let's get this over with."

Tiffany laughs with an annoyingly high-pitched voice. I'm at the end of my rope here with all the stress and fear, and she has to annoy me to no end. She deserves an award all right. Award for being the peskiest cunt out there. Is she wasted or is it just her everyday cuntness?

"I'm glad you enjoy our little show," I say, turning to Tiffany. I can see she won't be of any help. "I don't know if you heard it, but Michael is holding Chloe captive for something he wants from me, but I have no idea what it is. We came here to find out if you have any information about Michael's plans."

The icky smile she's been sporting freezes on her face, and her eyes flit around in fear. "Why do you think I might know something? I haven't talked to Michael since he ended our relationship."

"You must pardon Tiffany," Zane interrupts. "By 'relationship,' she means the same agreement you signed with Michael."

I roll my eyes at his silly explanation. Of course she meant that. How else would Michael be in a relationship with a woman? "How long did the *relationship* last?" I stress the word to irritate Zane. If he's acting like a jerk, why shouldn't I?

"He wanted me for a full year but it ended abruptly after only two months."

"Did you get paid?"

"No, but he promised me a role in a blockbuster that earned me my Oscar."

That's as good as cash in my book. "He fulfilled his part of the agreement but he didn't keep you for the full year."

She nods. "That's right."

"Do you know why? Did he start dating another woman?" I ask.

"No. I was his last girlfriend before you." She's more cooperative than I gave her credit for. Which means I should go ahead with the harder questions.

Taking a deep breath, I glance up at Ace. He remains still like a robot, except for his eyes staring back at me with concern. Perhaps he sees my hesitation, that's why he squeezes my hand gently below the table as an encouragement.

It is better that I die of embarrassment for asking the questions in my mind than miss a useful piece of information. So, I straighten up in my chair, push my shoulders back, and let my tongue take over. "Did Michael ever imply in any way that he'd expect you to service his business associates ... sexually?"

Tiffany's now-wide eyes dart between Zane and me as she sips from her glass of wine, likely wondering if I'm joking. It feels like a year passes until she pulls the glass away from her lips and places it back on the table. "Never. My relationship with him was strictly formal. Besides, it wasn't in the contract."

I stifle the need to roll my eyes at her suggestion. Who in his right mind would put such a term in a written contract unless he wants to get into trouble with the law? "Did you witness anything unusual or suspicious while you were with him?"

"Look, I wish I knew the information you're seeking, and I wish I could help Chloe, but I have neither heard nor witnessed anything about your current state with Michael. Also, Michael isn't the bad guy you make him out to be. He'll never hurt his daughter."

Both Ace and Zane chuckle at her words. I can see it clearly; she's acting diplomatically. Even if she knows something, relevant or not, she won't share it. She'll appear to be helpful and cooperating, but that's the only thing I'll get out of her. Defeated, I grab Zane's glass of scotch and down the entire drink in one shot, letting it burn my throat.

"Let's go." I get to my feet, feeling my cheeks getting warm from the alcohol, and glance at Tiffany. "Thank you," I mutter under my breath, although she doesn't deserve any gratefulness for the couple of unnecessary sentences she uttered, and pull Ace's hand so he stands too.

"Is that it?" Zane says as Ace and I start to leave. "You're not joining us for the rest of the night? I have a humongous bed, big enough for three of us."

I hear Tiffany giggling, but my senses shut down when I realize Ace isn't holding my hand anymore. Just in the time it takes to turn around, I find Ace on top of Zane with his fist ready to bury into Zane's face. Tiffany screams with her squeaky voice. An acute force urges me to jump and grab Ace's hand before he can hurt Zane, and I push him away with all my strength. Balls of fire shoot from his ice-blue eyes, and he growls while breathing heavily. I'm fairly sure I've never seen a man this angry and it scares the crap out of me.

Ace jerks his hand up and points his index finger up. "Stay the fuck away from her."

Despite my terror, I launch my body in front of him as a shield, not for him but for others he might hurt and shove him toward the exit. A few patrons stare at us on our way out, most likely astonished by Ace's glowing red face. I barely hear the hostess wishing us a great rest of the night. I highly doubt I'll have anything great the rest of my days until I resolve the problem with Michael.

I fumble through the pocket of Ace's pants to get his car keys and settle behind the wheel. With his anger, he'll likely drive us into a construction hole or something as detrimental. He doesn't open his mouth, doesn't even move his lips, as we drive back to his condo, just keeps that deadly stare on his face. Although his jealousy is baseless—I already had sex with Zane, and there's a sex tape of us likely to go viral one of these days—I keep my thoughts to myself.

Besides, if my intuition wasn't completely wrong again, Ace must have had something with Tiffany too, and she flirted with him. Did I throw a tantrum? No. Did I try to get into a fight or punch her? Hell no, and it doesn't matter if I considered it or not.

My ex never got territorial against me, and I thought it'd be romantic if he did every once in a while. Now, I'm not sure if anything about coming close to punching someone out of jealousy is good.

Ace still looks rigid by the time we get to his condo. His otherwise full lips are a thin line, and his nostrils flare each time he breathes. I have no idea what the protocol is for treating an angry man. Shall I leave him by himself until he gets it out of his system? Maybe distracting him with some silly conversation or a gentle hug will make the process go faster? I go for the latter and hug him as soon as we're in his living room. His hands remain at his sides for some time.

I draw circles on his back with the tips of my fingers, leave wet kisses on his throat and chin, and rub my chest against his, all to calm him down. And eventually, he softens and wraps his heavy arms around me.

"You won't talk to him anymore." He gazes down at my face with a threatening expression.

"You know I can't promise that," I whisper the truth softly, even though I know I should be more cautious. The truth is I know so little about Ace, I can't even estimate how violent he can get when angry. For all I know, he's an abusive man beneath his angel face.

"He uses women for his pleasure and treats them like a piece of dirt. He's a man-whore."

"I know. He works in a brothel, remember?"

My little joke takes away the last drops of his anger, and he lowers his head to steal a kiss from my lips. Feeling grateful that he's not an abuser but just concerned about my wellbeing, I let him devour me, his lips a little rougher than usual but otherwise passionate.

"I'm still not convinced he's being honest about his role in Michael's plans," Ace says, his lips brushing my own. "Be careful with the information you share with him."

"I will. What did he mean with you screwing all the women he'd slept with being typical of you?

Did you sleep with Tiffany?"

Inhaling deeply, he moves back, drops his hands by his sides, and nods.

The thought of Ace with Tiffany on the same bed I slept with him on turns my stomach upside down. "Anyone else?" *Besides me, of course.*

"Some girl he claimed he was in love with. Sally McNeal. I had no idea he was involved with her, otherwise I wouldn't have touched her. She approached me at a party Michael organized and openly told me she wanted to have sex with me. It's hard for a man to turn down an open sex invitation, you know?"

"No, I don't know." I allow myself a little fury although it's irrational. It's in his past, but it still hurts. That must be how he feels about Zane and me. "What happened then?"

"Well, we did it ... in one of the rooms in Michael's house, where he held the party. I don't know how, but Zane showed up in the room all of a sudden and started hitting me and yelling at me. Then, Michael came with his men and threw me out of the house. That's how I ended up moving to this condo."

"Oh, that happened when you were

eighteen?"

"Yeah, but I was legally an adult."

"That doesn't count." I move toward him and lace our bodies together. "How old was the cunt? She probably used you to make Zane jealous, but you wound up getting hurt in the end."

"It wasn't too bad after all. I'm happier now than ever not living under the same roof with Michael."

"I can certainly understand that."

My phone buzzes in my bag, and I untangle my arms from Ace to catch the call before it's too late.

"Hello," I answer without looking at the Caller ID. Anger is sneaking back at Ace's face. He must be thinking it's Zane calling me.

"Lindsay, it's Edrick. Hope I'm not disturbing you, but I have to remind you of the meeting in the marketing department at eight-thirty on the dot tomorrow. Michael won't be attending but you should be there to oversee the new account the department is taking over."

"Seriously? Am I still working at Hawkins Media Group?" Edrick must have known about my latest conversation with Michael, including his intention to sell me to his associates. I faintly remember Edrick's words about Michael's admirable work ethic when it comes to his business. He's as dirty a liar as Michael. And I'm a fool for believing them.

"The contract you signed with Michael is still in place. You're expected to continue your duties and responsibilities just like any other employee at HMG."

Yeah, right. Like the other employees are forced to satisfy some filthy men's sexual desires, too.

"So, you'll be there?" Edrick asks when I don't respond.

"Do I have another choice?" I disconnect and throw the phone together with my purse over at an armchair and plop down on the couch. "Looks like I have to go to work," I say to Ace as he takes his place next to me. "Maybe it's not too bad, though. I'll ask around about Michael. I might even get lucky and find out something useful."

"Don't," Ace says. "Michael will know it the second you open your mouth. His people aren't the ones you should trust."

"Then, how am I supposed to find out what he's up to?" I lean back and rest my head on the back of the couch. A feeling of exhaustion runs through my body, forcing my eyes closed. I'm trapped and drained out of my resources, and there's no one, other than myself, who can help me out.

*

After a short night of restless sleep, I take a quick stop at my apartment to change into a black skirt suit and drive to work. Although Ace offers to come with me, I politely decline and promise to meet him at his place after work. As sweet and protective as he is, I have to face my demons myself.

The meeting goes uneventfully, although I'd consider it high on the stressful scale in other circumstances, but now that I'm faced with the possibility of being a sex slave, the definition of stressful has changed in my life.

After the meeting, I take my place in my cubicle and fire up my computer to work on the data I'm supposed to finish by the end of the day. How delightful my day would have been if this data were the only thing I have to wrestle with, but I have my ass to protect and a person to save.

That's why I can't really sit around and work on the damn project the entire day. My fingers are itching to set up a meeting with Edrick, although he's probably the last person I should try to squeeze information out of. But who knows? Anyone is prone to a slip of the tongue every now and then.

Just when I start to get to my feet, my phone rings with an incoming text. I sit back in my chair and tab on the screen of my phone. A message from an unknown number reads: *"Meet me at the deli across the street in ten minutes."*

Who the hell is the text from?

Despite my suspicion and annoyance, my curiosity wins and I gather my jacket and purse and head out to the elevators. Curiosities seem like the highlights of my day because I stumble upon Edrick in the elevator as the doors slide open.

He nods at me curtly, with a distant smile playing on his lips, and moves to the side to give me space.

"Is Michael in? I'd like to talk with him for a couple of minutes," I say, although I know he's not in town.

"I'm afraid you can't." Edrick's tone is

spiteful yet calm. "He's out of the country for business and won't be back until the weekend. There's nothing to talk about anyway. You should know everything you're supposed to know."

There's no point in posing as if I'm not aware of what's going on. "So, you knew about his plans all along?"

His answer comes in the form of a smirk. "Did you seriously think that amount of money would be only for a couple of dates here and there?"

I did, actually. How stupid of me. "I guess money makes people blind."

He turns to me, and I look up at his face to see his friendly, casual self again. "Look, it's not the end of the world. You'll have a few bumps along the road, but when all is finished, you'll leave with almost two million dollars in your bank account and unbelievable fame that can take you anywhere you want."

Money and fame can eat my shit. "How about Chloe? Is he going to hurt her?"

"Michael has never been easy on his children, especially Chloe. But, as long as you do as he orders, he won't touch her. And, never ever try to involve police in this matter again. You won't get anywhere with it, and it'll just make him more upset."

I roll my eyes. "I learned my lesson. I just wish I knew Chloe was fine."

"Sorry, hun, but I can't give you that information unless Michael allows me to."

The elevator doors open with a ding, and I step out alongside Edrick. He smiles at me before turning in the opposite direction. I glance at my watch and realize it's already eleven minutes after I received the text. Hoping my mysterious date hasn't given up on me, I hasten out and cross the street.

There's a Subway and a local deli next to an Italian restaurant. Having no idea what my date looks like, or even if it's a man or a woman, I pull the door to the deli and scan the tables for my date. Only two tables are occupied, one by a women in her thirties with a teenage boy, and the other by a man in a black tie suit. The possibility of the man being my mysterious texter is higher than the mother with a son. So I move forward to his table.

He's focused on his laptop, drinking coffee,

and glances up at me with a surprised expression when I stand by his chair. He must be working for Michael, although his face is unfamiliar to me. Or perhaps, he's from our competition and will try to take advantage of my status as Michael's girlfriend and try to get information out of me. It might not be too bad to have *friends* who have the same hatred of Michael as me.

"Hello, I'm Lindsay," I say, hoping he'll take over the talking and save me from this uncomfortable situation.

"Hello, Lindsay." He smiles and his eyes roam all over me.

A hand grabs my back and I spin on my heels to see who's holding me. My jaw drops with surprise when I realize it is Tiffany, wearing a blonde wig and sunglasses. The black-suit man isn't the owner of the mysterious text?

"Is she your friend?" the guy asks, but both Tiffany and I ignore him, moving to the back of the deli, and sit at a table for two.

"Thanks for coming," Tiffany whispers, leaning toward me and rubbing her hands together over the table. "I came to apologize for my behavior yesterday. I was a little drunk and there was no way I could talk about Michael when under the same roof with two of his men."

"He had men following you?"

"Not me, but Zane and most likely Ace too. I can recognize them easily. They always wear a leather jacket."

I look around to see if any man with a leather jacket is around.

"It's like their uniform. So silly of them to have themselves easily spotted like that. Anyway, I hope you didn't think I was very rude to you yesterday."

"If it's why you came here, don't worry. Your apology is accepted," I say.

"It's not the only thing I came here for."

I move forward on the table to hear what she has to say, my nerves on a high alert because I know something big is coming. A waitress interrupts us, but as soon as we order coffee, she leaves us alone.

"Yesterday you asked me if Michael expected me to service his business associates sexually."

"Yes," I say to push her to continue."

"Well, he didn't, but I think it was only a

matter of time if I'd stayed as his girlfriend."

"How do you know that?"

"I know someone who works for him and has to attend to his clients' needs that way as a part of her job duties."

"Who?"

"His secretary, Julie Meadow."

"Really?" My eyes widen with surprise, and suddenly I feel guilty for looking down on Julie on my first day at HMG headquarters.

"Yeah. She had no idea about it when she took up the job as his secretary, and now there's no way she can quit her job because she knows too much."

Yet another person suffering at Michael's hands. Does it surprise me? No.

The waitress shows up with our coffee and the bill. Both Tiffany and I ignore the drinks.

"There's something else you should know," Tiffany whispers as soon as the waitress disappears. I feel a shiver going through my torso with the serious tone of her voice. Something big is coming. I can feel it deep in the fibers of my body. "Last year, about two months into my contract with Michael, I was accompanying him to an event in New York. The morning after the event, he got a phone call that made him terribly upset. I stayed in the same suite with him, that's why I could listen to the conversation."

"What was it about?" I hold my breath, not even daring to move my eyes.

"It was about a video on YouTube and he literally spent three hours on the phone to get it deleted. Can you guess which video it was?"

I feel blood draining out of my limbs, and my arms fall on each side of my body with shock. "The video I was in. The iron slap?" It's a confirmation about all my suspicions about Michael. What he wants from me is beyond some sex slavery.

"Exactly. I checked the dates last night to make sure I was right. The video was online on YouTube right after the kidnapping of your sister and you. But Michael made sure nobody saw it in those first weeks. I don't know why it is so important to him, but I've never seen a man so furious in my life as I witnessed Michael when he received that phone call about the video. I literally feared for my life. It was also the day he canceled my contract with him. I can only imagine how much more upset he must have gotten when the video popped up again after two months. He couldn't stop it that second time around."

"Do you have any idea why that video got him so worked up?" I can barely blurt out the words.

She shakes her head. "I'm sorry. That's the only information I have about Michael. I have to go now before one of his men finds out I'm talking to you. Call me at the number I texted you with if you need any help, although I don't think I can offer much. Good luck with everything." She pats me on my shoulder gently and leaves while I stare at the wall across from me with my mouth popped open.

Can she be lying to lead me into the wrong direction? But, she was right about one thing. The Iron Slap video didn't go viral immediately afterward. Now that I think about it, it took a little over two months before it became popular. Not just that, the kidnapping itself made it to headlines in all major newspapers both print and online after two months too. Did Michael also try to stop the news from spreading?

What could be in that damned video that has turned him against me? That I killed a murderer with just the slap of my hand? Wait a minute …

Can Michael be related to Macey Williams? If that's the case, he's now trying to take his revenge on me. But why the hell then would he try to hide the video from the public? To honor his relative's dignity?

This new information might not have brought me any closer to Michael's plans, but it sure opened Pandora's box with tons of new questions filling up my mind. And I don't even know how I will use it.

The Video - ACE

After I drop Lindsay at work, I head to Pleasure Extraordinaire but can hardly focus on the tasks, so I leave Alexander as my substitute and take the day off to do some research. My first stop is Diana's home. I pulled her into this mess when I asked for her help to host my sister at her place while she recovered from Michael's last brutality.

The door to her condo is unlocked; a subtle

message from Michael to inform me that he was here. I step inside the neat living room and inhale deeply in an effort to catch a scent of my sister. Neither Diana, nor Chloe deserves to be manhandled by Michael or his men, but that's what they must be going through every minute until someone saves them. That someone hopefully being me.

I check the bedrooms and sit on the bed where Chloe was supposed to spend the night. Her phone is lying on the vanity alongside a jacket and a purse. I wonder if she even made it to the bed before Michael's men kidnapped her. Probably not. If I thought the police could help, I wouldn't hesitate to give them a detailed account of the events leading up to Chloe and Diana's kidnapping, but if Lindsay's experience at the police station is a sign of anything, it's that Michael has arms and ears in every local police station.

I go through the open suitcase at the foot of the bed with the hope of finding something useful among silk and cotton, but stumble upon a picture of Chloe, Irene, and me taken in a restaurant on Irene's thirty-eighth birthday. It was one of the handful of occasions where Michael didn't hover

over us, or Zane didn't ruin the moment with his capriciousness.

I was very lucky having a woman like Irene as my mother, loving me as her own child despite the fact that I was adopted to cover up Michael's homosexuality. She had love for everyone, even for Michael. But she didn't have the power to leave him, and among us all, she was the only one who could have. She could have divorced him and ended his sadistic acts on us, but she never was able to. Instead, she chose to take her life and leave us alone and vulnerable in Michael's hands.

Michael ruined my mother, and now he's onto Chloe. Maybe he won't kill her, but it doesn't take a rocket scientist to know he'll do irrevocable damage to her, both physically and emotionally. What will I do if Chloe too chooses to follow Irene's steps and kills herself? Will I be able to survive losing another person who I love and couldn't protect?

My disturbing thoughts come to a halt with the buzzing of my phone.

"We need to talk ASAP!" the text from Lindsay says. I delete it immediately, although Michael's people must have read it already if they're monitoring my phone. I slip the picture of me with Chloe and Irene into the pocket of my jacket with my phone and leave the apartment.

Hurrying out of the building, I get into my car in the parking lot in the basement, but as I start the engine, someone knocks on the window beside me. I roll it down and see Dylan Berenson, Chloe's fiancé.

"What are you doing here?" He's one of the people who saw Chloe being beaten up by Michael, and like all of us, he couldn't stop him either.

"Can we talk?"

"Sure." I unlock the doors and watch him round the front of the car and climb into the passenger seat. "What are you doing here?"

"I was worried about Chloe. She kicked me out of her apartment after the ... But I couldn't leave. I waited in front of her apartment building and then saw you going in and coming out with her. I followed you here."

"Michael had her kidnapped."

"Fuck it, I know."

"How? Do you know where they took her? They took my friend too."

He shakes his head. "Unfortunately, no. I saw

them taking the girls and pushing them into a black van. I even followed them until I-5 then lost them."

"Did you get the license plate number?"

He shifts in the seat to get his phone out of his pocket, fumbles with it for a few seconds before handing it to me. I glance at him then at the phone, and almost drop the damn thing when I see the photos of Chloe and Diana being hauled into a black van by four men who look like they just broke out of prison. There was also two close-ups of the plate number. I could go to police with these pictures to have Chloe located if I wasn't sure Michael would find out my intention the minute I enter the station.

After sending the photos to my phone, I give it back to Dylan.

"What are we gonna do?" he asks.

I shrug because I don't have a fucking clue how we can go about it.

"I'll be waiting here..." Dylan says with a sad note evident in his voice. Does he really love Chloe? I thought their affair was only a show for the media and Michael.

"No point in wasting your time here. Michael

won't send them back. We'll have to find them."

"I don't know what else to do." He looks ready to burst into tears, and I notice bruises around his neck. Michael or his men must have strangled him last night while they forced him to watch how Michael beat up Chloe. What a fucked up situation this is.

"Come with me," I say and without further explanation, I head to my apartment, hoping Lindsay is waiting for me there. Bringing Dylan might not be the best of the ideas, especially considering the possibility that he might be working for Michael, but I so desperately want to believe that people like Michael come only in a handful, one in maybe hundreds of thousands, and Dylan doesn't belong to that group, and he genuinely loves my sister. If he really feels how he looks, lost and beaten after losing my sister, then he deserves to be part of my little circle of people I trust.

I unlock and open the door to my condo and find Lindsay pacing back and forth across the living room. As soon as she sees me, she jumps to my side and hugs me tightly. The softness of her body helps relax my agitated nerves, and I lower my head to nuzzle her hair. She's so small in my arms, almost breakable, but I know beneath her fragile figure lies a strong woman, and she's with me in this. Not being alone in my fight against Michael for the first time feels so strangely comforting and makes me believe we might actually have a chance against him.

"I learned something important, but I don't know what it..." She stops mid-sentence, likely because she's noticed Dylan behind me.

"Lindsay, do you remember Dylan, Chloe's fiancé?"

"Of course I do. Hello, Dylan." She moves away from me to shake hands with Dylan. I close the door and follow them to the living room under Lindsay's questioning eyes. She must be telepathically asking me why the hell I've brought him here when she has an important piece of information to share.

I nod my answer. "We can trust Dylan."

She rolls her eyes when Dylan isn't looking in her direction and shakes her head almost invisibly.

"I swear I'm not working for Michael," Dylan says to support my conviction. "He ruined my family's business. Besides, I love Chloe. She's the love of my life. I was a piece of garbage for letting

LIV BENNETT

Michael attack her last night, but I learned my
lesson. I'll protect her no matter what. I'll do
anything to save her. This waiting, not knowing
anything, is killing me."

"What is it you found out?" I ask to urge
Lindsay to talk.

She shoots me one of her 'What the fuck?'
looks but eventually gives in. "I talked with Tiffany
again." She turns around, heading toward the
couch. My eyes immediately fall on her firm ass
beneath the tight skirt she's wearing. I can barely
focus on her words when she wiggles her hips like
that.

"Wait a minute. Did you say Tiffany? Tiffany
Jordan?" I ask.

"Yeah." She cocks her head to eye me
suspiciously.

"When did you talk to her?"

"Today, about an hour ago. She didn't want
to talk yesterday because of Zane and two men in
the restaurant she suspected worked for Michael."

"What did she say?" I ask.

"Michael terminated the contract with her
the day after the incident with Macey Williams.

According to Tiffany, he tried to stop the video of me killing Macey Williams from spreading. That's why the video showed up two months after the incident and not immediately afterwards."

"What could be in that video?"

"I don't know, but I think the reason for my recruitment lies in it. I'm almost sure about it."

"What video?" Dylan asks.

"The video of Iron Slap," I reply and Lindsay laughs bitterly.

"Don't tell me you haven't seen it, because you'd be the only person who hasn't watched that damn video," Lindsay says.

Dylan sits at the left end of the couch, nodding. "I saw it. Only once, though. The part with Mrs. Garnett giving birth to her dead child... ahh... It was horrible."

"Tell me about it." Lindsay takes off her jacket, neatly places it on a chair and then plops down on the couch on the other end.

My cock stirs at the sight of her silky skin exposed by the collar of her shirt and I instantly regret having invited Dylan. "What do we do now? Shall we watch the video again?" I ask to distract my uncontrollable urges.

"I don't think I can stomach to watch it again," Dylan says.

I switch on the TV anyway, hook up my phone to it, and find the video online. Pulling a chair next to Lindsay, I tab start the video. The images look all the more stomach-churning on the large screen.

Lindsay's sister, Taylor Garnett, coming down the stairs, screaming for Lindsay, Macey Williams shooting Annette Greene right in the mouth. Taylor Garnett fainting with shock ... Macey Williams preparing to shoot her second victim ... Lindsay getting up and smashing Macey right into the hook.

Lindsay's face in the video is one of the most horrifying sights I've ever seen in my life, only after Michael's when he's outraged. Fortunately, Lindsay's outrage came from the motivation to protect her sister and the other victim from a bloody murderer, not like Michael who has nothing motivating him but the evil in his black heart.

The video gets all the more tormenting when Lindsay holds her dead niece in her arms, and then hands her to Taylor. Lindsay cries while watching Taylor clutch her baby against her chest, and I turn away to avoid both scenes. It must be the worst moment in the world for Taylor—being kidnapped, witnessing a murder, and losing her own child. All at the same time.

"I'm very sorry for Mrs. Garnett," Dylan says. "I met her at the engagement party. A very classy lady."

"Also the nicest person you can ever meet," Lindsay says, brushing the tears from her cheeks. "She donated over a hundred million dollars to free clinics in L.A."

"Is that true?" I ask, hating the fact that my voice trembles.

"Yeah. Michael didn't refrain from using that information to threaten me. If I don't follow his orders, he'll cancel the construction project he has with Taylor. If he goes ahead with his threat, Taylor's company will suffer big time, and because she donated most of her money, she won't have the finances to back it up until they find new business to sustain them."

It's not surprising to hear that Michael has Lindsey so firmly in his clutches.

Dylan ruffles his hair and turns to look at Lindsay. I can't say I'm very comfortable with him sitting so close to my girl. "I'd never heard of that kind of birth defect until I saw Mrs. Garnett's baby in the video. Did it run in the family?" he asks.

What a dumb remark to make.

"No," Lindsay snaps.

"Sorry, I didn't mean it that way. I was just curious."

"We don't know why it happened to her. Even if she survived, she wouldn't be able to see, hear, or feel anything. Babies born with Anencephaly die within a few hours of birth." Lindsay says, fidgeting with her fingers, gazing down at her skirt. Her voice falters, and I'm afraid she'll start crying again. I reach over and grab her hand and pull it to my lips to kiss it. She glances up at me, eyes already glittering with tears.

"What in the video could have caused Michael to get all defensive and make him try to hide it from public view?" I ask in an effort to prevent Lindsay from bursting into tears.

She blinks several times and wipes her eyes with her other hand.

"Can it be about the other people in the

video?" I ask again.

"That was my first thought, too. Perhaps he knew Macy Williams and tried to protect her name. Have you heard of her before? Could she have been Michael's relative or an acquaintance?"

"If she was, I have no way to know. Michael never introduced me to his relatives."

"Zane might know."

Fuck. Not Zane again. I hate the fact that he's always the first person that pops in Lindsay's mind whenever she needs help. But, I should curb my jealousy so we can find out the truth. Especially because she's right in her observation. Zane, both being Michael's biological son and much older than me, has a better chance to know Michael's extended family and relatives than I ever will.

"Maybe it was just about Mrs. Garnett," Dylan points out. "She's running the construction project with Michael. Maybe he just didn't want his contractor's name making the headlines all over the nation."

"Although it doesn't make any sense at all, you might be right," Lindsay says. "Just like his efforts to hide his homosexuality don't make sense either."

"What? Is Michael gay?" Dylan jerks his head to look at me.

"Oops." Lindsay gives me an apologetic smile, as if I give a damn shit about who knows Michael's sexual tendencies.

"Don't worry. He signed an NDA," I say anyway to calm Lindsay down.

"I wasn't going to tell anyone anyway. I'm just shocked. That's all," Dylan says. "So, you're posing as his girlfriend, but not actually dating him. Is that it?"

Lindsay nods and gets to her feet, leaning down to brush her lips against mine. Before I can even get a chance to devour her lips, she places a quick, dry kiss on my lips, and straightens up. "I gotta go. My lunch break was over about ten minutes ago. People must have already started wondering where I'm hiding."

"How about the land?" Dylan doesn't seem to be willing to end our talk. "Can it be about the land he stole from my father and is now converting to the home development project with Mrs. Garnett's construction company?"

Lindsay freezes, staring at the blank TV ahead of her. Dylan's point isn't without merit, actually. The land and the construction project are the reason Michael got acquainted with Taylor Garnett, and through her, with Lindsay.

"Didn't your father sell the land to Michael willingly?" I ask.

"Fuck no. The land belonged to us for three generations, from my great-grandfather to my father. I was going to inherit it, then my sons, and the sons of my sons. There was no talk about selling it ever, until Michael started with his dirty tricks. In a matter of six months, one of the most profitable country clubs in the state wound up bankrupt all because of Michael's intrigues. My father had no choice other than to sell it for half of what it was worth so he could cover the debts and save us from poverty."

Lindsay glances at her watch with a concerned look on her face. "Okay, all very interesting questions, but I really have to go."

I get up, grab her jacket, holding it for her to put it on, and then slide my arm around her waist while walking her to the door. She twirls on her heels and plasters her soft body against mine at the doorway, pulling my head down to face me up close. "Aren't you going back to work, too?"

I shake my head and lean forward to lick her lips softly. She purrs into my mouth, ignoring Dylan's presence only a few feet away, and I tighten my hold around her body. "I'll be waiting for you. Don't take too long at work."

"I won't," she whispers in my ear, raising the hair on my neck with the seduction in her voice, and pulls back. I remain staring after her long after she's gone and swallow down the strange lump of loneliness forming in my throat. She'll be gone for at least five hours, and I have no fucking idea how I'll kill those hours until she's back in my arms again.

"I should probably get going too." Dylan appears beside me as I'm staring at the empty hallway. "I'll ask my father if he knows someone who can track down the van Chloe was kidnapped with."

"Keep me updated if you find out anything."

"You too, man. We're a team now."

I nod and shake hands with him. Once, I was just one person against Michael, now I have a team of three. Can we succeed? Stop Michael's violence and get back my sister without any of us getting hurt? If we can, I can't even begin to imagine how my life will be without Michael's ever-controlling presence. But if we fail or someone gets hurt in the process or even dies, I don't have the slightest idea how I will be able to handle it.

The Gossip

The employees of Hawkins Media Group must have signed a secret pact to make work a living hell for me. From the girl at the front desk to my cubicle neighbor, Liz, whom I had a delightful lunch with just on Friday, everyone seems to have sworn to give me the stink eye without any attempt to be subtle about it. No hi's or how-are-you's, not even asking which button to push in the elevator. Only obvious glares.

What's wrong with these people? Did they receive a memo about the problem between Michael and me so they're collectively punishing me, pushing me to the edge to see how far my patience can stretch? I'd be pleased to show them the consequences of trying my limits if I wasn't hell-bound after Michael.

Liz not only glares at me as I take my place at my desk, but also murmurs between her teeth something incomprehensible but annoying enough to keep me from concentrating on my work. After several minutes, I finally give up and turn to her, and say, not in a really friendly tone, "I'm burning to hear the reason why you can't take your eyes off me today."

I see the other employees turn their heads. Liz smirks and shoves her curly black hair over her shoulder. "Rumors have it that you're burning for a whole lot of other reasons too."

"What does that mean? What rumors are you talking about?"

"You and Zane Hawkins. I shouldn't be surprised at how quickly you could wind up in both men's beds. A quick help from Google shows you're no stranger to seducing high-level executives. I pity the idiot you fooled in your previous job, but Michael Hawkins is no airhead like your previous lover. He'll know how to put your little trailer-trash ass out the door when he comes back from his business trip. You're no different than a prostitute, just a little smarter."

"What the fuck are you talking about?" I jerk on my feet and leap the distance between us to get to her desk, ignoring the curious stares of the others in the office. The anger in my voice and on my face must have scared Liz because she leans back in her chair and lifts her arms to her face to protect herself. I inhale deeply to calm myself down and keep my arms close to my body where they can't hurt anyone. She doesn't know the truth, I tell myself. She has no way to know Zane tricked me into it, and Michael is probably the most dangerous man on the entire East Coast. "Who told you those lies?" I lower my head to get close to her face.

She clears her throat and stares at me through her crossed arms. "Julie Meadow."

Michael's secretary? The hooker herself, huh! Maybe she's not as innocent as Tiffany made her out to be for having been forced to serve Michael's clients sexually.

As if Julie's bad-mouthing isn't enough for

me to lose my integrity in the eyes of my colleagues, Zane has to show up with an utterly annoying insidious smile on his face to complete my picture as the personal hooker of the HMG's executives. The fact that I actually slept with two Hawkins brothers doesn't help my conscious, either.

"Hey, babe," he mumbles in what I think he thinks is a seductive way but my stomach comes close to expulsing the little amount of sandwich I ate during lunch. More so for hearing Liz snort.

"I'm not a fucking babe. Who do you think you are, spreading lies about me?" Well, it's actually Julie, but she wouldn't open her mouth if she didn't get the green light from Zane or Michael.

"What's going on?" He strolls toward me, his body swaying left and right like a boat against violent waves, and I smell a hint of alcohol on his breath as he stops before me. I could have dealt with him if he were sober, but I have no interest in trying to talk sense into him while he's drunk so he can save me from this hairy situation. For all I know, he might blurt out the truth about the afternoon in my condo. My colleagues already believe Julie's lies, they don't need further proof to label me as the HMG's hooker.

"Why did you come?" I take a step back to escape his alcohol breath and also because he's invading my personal space.

"I need to talk to you."

"Okay, say what you want to say now." Crossing my arms, I glance down at Liz and hope Zane is here for a work-related reason.

"Why Ace?" he murmurs lowly, but I guess everyone in the office has heard him.

"Oh, God!" I grab him by the elbow and drag him out until we stop at the elevator. When he starts to open his mouth again, I hush him with a glare. We enter the elevator and don't speak a word until the cab stops at the floor of his office. I make sure not to show any anger as we stride to his office.

His secretary informs Zane of an upcoming meeting in a half hour and nods at me. I return her gesture and walk through the glass doors of Zane's office. As he heads to his desk, I pour him a cup of coffee without sugar or cream so he can at least get a clear head. I spot a bottle of whiskey and a dirty glass beside it. Why the hell is he drinking on a work day? Just like a spoiled child, behaving badly as soon as the parents aren't around to discipline him... Is that how he's taking advantage of Michael's absence; by getting wasted rather than get some work done?

"Why Ace, huh?" he repeats when I place the cup of coffee in front of him. "What do you, women, even find in that retarded piece of shit?"

I shake my head in disapproval of his words and settle on the chair across from him. "Watch your mouth. He's your brother."

"A reason why you shouldn't be with him. Do you get off fucking brothers? Is that your thing?"

"Oh shut up and drink your coffee."

One good thing about drunken men is that they follow orders. Zane sips his warm beverage slowly but steadily until the whole cup is empty. I can see the sense is coming back to his face.

"Lindsay, you're driving me crazy. I thought we had chemistry."

"Oh, please, like chemistry is enough. Besides, I didn't come to your office to talk about it. I need your help with something else."

"Uh-huh, yeah, why should I help you?"

"Because it's related to your sister. I need you

to be completely honest with me. Do you know why Michael hired me? If I know the reason, maybe I can find a way to negotiate with him so he releases Chloe."

"I've got nothing to say. I'm not his confidant. He never shares his plans with me, including the work matters. I usually find out his business strategies at the same time as the other employees."

"Are you telling the truth? I don't want to believe you can sit here doing nothing while your sister is being hurt."

"I'm honest with you, Lindsay. I want that jackass to release my sister more than you do."

I pause to think how I should proceed about the talk I had with Tiffany earlier today. As much as I want to consider Zane on my side, rather than Michael's, I have to take into account the probability that he's with Michael for the sake of Tiffany. "Do you know if Macey Williams is in any way related to Michael?"

He raises an eyebrow. "How did you come to that conclusion?"

"That's not important. Just answer my question. Do you have any idea if Michael knew

Macey Williams?"

"Are you speculating that Michael hired you to avenge Macey Williams?"

"I don't know. The only thing I know is that he tried to prevent the video of Iron Slap from spreading for about two months. I'm suspecting it's all about Macey."

"She wasn't a relative, fortunately. And if she was a friend of Michael's, I have no idea. The same goes for the two other women in the video."

I tab my fingers on the arms of the chair in disappointment. I was half expecting Zane wouldn't provide me with full information, but he didn't give me any reason to doubt him either.

"Are you together with him? Ace?" Zane asks, his expression frustrated.

"I kind of am, yes."

"You know it'll be damaging for your reputation. Openly dating Michael, getting laid by me, and now hooking up with Ace. If Michael goes ahead with his threat, I'll have no reason to keep your name clean as long as you're with Ace."

"I'm well aware of the complications of my situation, and thank you for your concern but..."

"But?" he asks.

"You don't want to hear that."

"I do."

"I really like Ace."

Zane glances at me blankly for a brief second before throwing his head back and starting to laugh loudly. I shake my head in disbelief and get to my feet.

He yells behind me as I open the door, "I'm giving you two weeks until you see his true colors. But don't worry; I'll be here waiting for you."

What the fuck? He must still be drunk for contemplating us having something together. He can't possibly think I'll happily accommodate him and his female friends' sexual needs.

The rest of the afternoon passes with my dear colleagues' low murmurs, giggles, and narrow-eyed stares. After a few minutes of being disturbed by their rudeness, I decide to ignore them, and from that moment on, I start feeling more relaxed and can actually focus on my work for two straight hours. Nothing like the motivation of being hated by colleagues to get work done. It reminds me of the last months at my previous job and how my then colleagues sided against me and blamed me for seducing my boss. I did most of the work on the team while they spent their work hours gossiping about me.

Before leaving, I open up my company email account and start an email addressed to Julie Meadow.

"A little bird whispered to my ears that you cater to Michael's business partners' needs a little more than would be customary. If you don't put an end to your smear campaign against me, I know just whom I will share that little secret with."

The fact that my message is written and can be used against me should prove to her that I don't fear her and that should be enough to scare her off for the moment. I collect my purse, jacket, and phone, and head off toward the exit with my chin up and chest forward. Despite what the world might think of me, I know the truth and I'll be damned if I allow any malicious person to get into my head.

My phone buzzes with an incoming message. It's from Edrick, saying that he needs me to sign a document before leaving. Rather than going downstairs, I take the elevator up to the executives' floor. Edrick, however, isn't in his office and his secretary has no idea about the document Edrick wants me to sign. It sounds suspiciously like a plan to test my patience. Forcing myself to smile at Edrick's secretary, I leave for Julie's office since she might be more knowledgeable about Edrick's whereabouts than his own secretary. Go figure.

I feel a little uncomfortable about meeting with Julie right after my unfriendly email, yet also curious to see how she'll react. I nod at the girl at the desk outside Julie's office before knocking on Julie's door.

After three raps, she doesn't answer me. However, she might be doing it on purpose. That's why I take the initiative and open the door, parting it slightly to see if she's sitting in there and simply ignoring me. I almost turn around to leave when I see her empty desk, but sounds coming from next door, from Michael's office, make me stop.

All of a sudden, Julie emerges behind the door, her long hair disheveled, her red lipstick smudged around her lips, and she's holding her hand on her chest, obviously trying to hold back her gag reflex. She doesn't realize I'm watching her and runs her hands through her hair, breathing in and out deeply, and straightening her skirt at the same time.

My mind goes through countless possibilities

about what she might have been doing in there and with whom. As far as I know, Edrick is gay, so he's off the list. It could be anyone though. The sky is her limit in this case. For all I know, Zane got too worked up by my rejection and tried to get his release using Julie. Although my respect for Julie is below zero for spreading rumors around about me, I admit that her situation is no different than me in terms of bowing to the abusive men around her for survival.

I clear my throat to announce my presence and see her startle at my guttural noise. Her face goes from shocked to dismay, and stays as embarrassed.

"Do you know where Edrick is?" I ask. "He told me I have to sign some document but his secretary doesn't know anything about it."

"Yes. It's somewhere here. Give me a sec." Her voice comes out low. She can't look into my eyes. The sight of her so vulnerable makes me feel guilty for sending her that email.

Michael's door opens again, and two dark-skinned and bearded men, wearing white head scarfs and long, white robes, stand at the doorway, eyeing me curiously. One speaks in a foreign language —Arabic, judging by their clothes— the other one simply nods and moves forward to the door I'm standing in front of and opens it without requesting me to move.

Bile rises in my throat as I notice the hungry eyes of the other guy sizing me up and down. Did Julie have to do anything sexual with them? Repulsive doesn't even begin to cover the feeling I'd have if I were forced to satisfy them sexually.

Finally the guy who's staring at me releases me from his disgusting gaze and turns to Julie. "Tell Mr. Hawkins that we would be very pleased to do business with him." He smiles at Julie mischievously before leaving with his friend.

I make it my mission not to speak a word about the two men with Julie, although I'm dying to know what they were doing here and why. Julie finds the document and hands it to me. She's clearly mortified, and I have no intention of making her more uncomfortable by staying longer, so I sign the document as soon as I realize it's related to the marketing project we've taken over and wish her a good evening before leaving.

I thought Michael is hostile to me because of the secret reason he hired me, but it seems it's his usual behavior toward everyone. He's an abuser, a bully for forcing his subordinates into activities that they haven't consented to do. I'm far beyond upset with him and can't wait for the day to come to take him down and end his tyranny.

The First Time

I unlock the front door of Ace's condo, still feeling the shock of receiving the key to his place so soon, and look around for him in the spacious rooms. When I realize he's not here, I throw myself on the couch for a quick nap. The stress of the day coupled with the sleepless night I had makes me drift into a deep sleep almost instantly.

As I wake up after half an hour, Ace is still not home. There is only one other place he can be and it's Pleasure Extraordinaire. After fixing my hair and makeup, I drive to his work with a feeling of discomfort accompanying me all throughout the way.

This will be the first time I'll be visiting Pleasure Extraordinaire as something other than a client. Actually, I'm not even sure if I'll be allowed to enter since officially I'm nothing to Ace. Just the girl he recently started screwing. A little voice in my head is whispering that he might not be genuinely into me, but just doing it for the sake of his sister. If that's indeed the truth, I'll be crushed after everything, in addition to the horror I'll go through at the upcoming weekend with Michael's Russian friends.

As I kill the engine in front of the Pleasure Extraordinaire building, a young boy, whom I've never seen before, opens the door. Another boy retrieves my car key and drives it off while I'm asked to wait at the entrance. From the giggling sounds coming at the either side of the door, I think the reason for my waiting is to prevent the other client and me from seeing each other. Might be for confidentiality reasons or simply to keep the spirits high by diminishing any shameful or discomforting feelings that meeting another client can cause.

I scan the over-sized garden to keep myself distracted, and when my escort gets the clear, he opens the door for me and again, I'm welcomed by a dozen men lined up at the entrance. But this time, I can't for the love of God find it in me to gaze at them. I should offer my deepest thanks to Ace for taking away my unusual appetite for men. I have no doubt his ego will be stroked if he ever finds out.

In front of Ace's office, I nod with a smile at my escort and knock on the door while watching him vanish down the long corridor. I don't hear any 'yes' or 'come in', but open the door anyway, and nearly drop down on my knees in shock, finding Laila giving Ace a sensual massage on his shoulders while he's settled at his desk. Then, the fact that he's fully clothed and reading a stack of papers squeezed in his hand registers in my brain.

"Hello, Seven," Laila chirps with her sweet voice accompanied by a lovely smile, but doesn't stop her hands from rubbing Ace's arms. She's wearing a low-cut, bright green dress that brings out the red of her hair and the blue of her eyes. Her skin glows as her cheeks flash pink. She's the definition of beauty and sensual, and obviously

Ace feels comfortable enough around her to let her touch him.

My heart fills with sadness as I remember the sight of Ace having sex with her while she moaned with ecstasy less than forty-eight hours ago. This is extraordinary because sadness is something I feel exclusively for Taylor or my dead mother. Anger is the defining emotion I feel toward everyone else. Has Ace scaled up to the category in my heart that is reserved only for my family?

Ace lifts his hand to touch Laila's and with that, she pulls her grip away and steps around his chair.

"Let me know if you need more help." She winks at Ace and offers me another of her beautiful smile as she leaves.

I move to the side to let her pass and stay still until she closes the door behind her. Ace stands and approaches me, and I let him hold me in his arms and even kiss me.

"I missed you," he whispers to my ear and nibbles on my earlobe. My hands move up his arms and wrap around his neck while I moan with the pleasure of having him so close to me. His hands wander across my back down to my ass until he cups me and pushes me against him.

I've missed him too, more than I allow myself to admit, and my heart feels like it's literarily going to crack in two with pain because now I see he's just like his brother, having numerous lovers he can enjoy anytime he wants. Tears gather in my eyes, and sobs choke up my throat as I pull him against me.

"Lindsay," I hear him whisper. "What's going on?" he asks when I don't respond.

I finally loosen my grip and pull back. My eyes are all wet with tears by now, and my makeup most likely ruined. I wipe my tears with my hand and turn my back against him so he doesn't witness my emotional breakdown.

He doesn't let me go, though, and runs his hands around my waist and lowers his head down to kiss my neck. "What's going on, babe?"

Babe? Just like Zane called me earlier. My stomach twists. How much more similar are they?

"Do you remember how you told me you didn't want me to fuck another man?"

"Hm-hm."

"It goes both ways."

He chuckles against my ear. His hands get rougher as they travel toward my breasts and he cups them like a bra. "Laila was only giving me a massage if that's what you're referring to."

"How would you like me getting a massage from ..." I don't finish the sentence on purpose. He might fill in the blank with JJ but most likely Zane will be the first man that will come to his mind.

He shifts his hands toward my hips and turns me around with a swift move. I barely register the anger on his face as he pushes me against the wall. "Laila is an employee. She has no influence over me whatsoever."

I narrow my eyes at him, examining his face for the truthfulness of his words, but when his face gives away nothing, I move ahead for concrete evidence of his words and grab his semi-hard penis beneath his black slacks.

"It's all for you, baby. I'm hard only for you," he defends himself under hooded eyes and bites his lower lip with intent.

"I don't believe you." I tighten my grip only to feel him get harder.

He shoves his hips against my palm and presses his hand over mine to apply more pressure against his cock. "All for you, baby."

I shake my head in disbelief and pull back my hand.

"You want proof? I'll give you one." He turns around, arranges a chair for me beside his desk, and signals for me to sit on it. I watch him suspiciously as we sit on our chairs at the same time, and then he unzips his slacks and releases his cock through the opening at the front of his boxer briefs. He looks all the more glorious with his hardness poking out of his clothes, and I gulp down and melt, trying to push away the images of how I can sit astride him on his chair and slide it inside me.

"Quit looking at me like that," Ace whispers, and I wonder what's on his mind. I roll my eyes and look the other way. The next time I glance at him — at his cock actually, because honestly it dominates everything else— his cock is all flaccid and small.

He reaches over to grab his phone and dials patiently, his one eyebrow raised all the while. "Can you come over for a minute?" is all he says before he hangs up. His face doesn't give anything away.

I shift and cross my legs, straightening my pencil skirt. It sure is getting warmer in here. I start to take off my jacket but stop when I'm confronted with Ace's disapproving look. He's shaking his head no. "You're not to take off any piece of clothing until I tell you to."

I guess we're back to cold and commanding Ace once again.

A faint knock on the door and Laila enters. Her sweet perfume hits my nostrils first, and I find myself evaluating her super-mini green dress that's hugging her sensual curves tightly.

"Hi boss. I didn't think you'd need me so soon," she speaks sweetly, batting her eyebrows. Honestly, if I'm affected by her beauty so much, what man wouldn't want her?

"Your help is always welcome, sweetheart, but Seven, here, would love to see you give a little dance. Would you mind cheering her up a little?" Ace grins and leans back in his seat, pushing himself closer to the desk just enough to hide his naked penis from Laila's view but keep it visible to me.

"Oh, God. Of course not." I glance back and forth at Ace and Laila. "I didn't ask for that. I don't want you to do anything for me. Please, just go back to your work and don't bother with Ace's silly suggestions."

"Your satisfaction is my work and pleasure too, Seven." Laila smiles at me and reaches for the top button of her dress. My eyes immediately drop at the lovely curves of her breasts. I am speechless as I watch her undo them one by one, revealing more of her milky-white body swaying slowly to the soft music that's just started.

"Jesus, please stop." I glare at Ace for putting me in such an inappropriate situation and making me watch a girl striptease, including the music and all. He points down at his still-flaccid cock with his chin, and in that instant I understand what his intentions are. He's trying to show me how little effect Laila has on him, well at least on his cock, because it's not getting hard although Laila has just dropped her dress onto the floor and is standing two feet away from me with a red lace bra and matching semi-transparent thong.

Either someone has turned down the AC or my body is producing too much heat for me to remain comfortable in my suit. Laila twirls around and lets the curls of her beautiful hair spread all over her shoulders. Shit, this girl has it all. Full breasts, curvy hips, flat stomach, long legs, and I, truly a straight woman, start feeling wetness pooling between my legs just watching her dance.

I whisper my fuck you's to Ace when Laila isn't looking and watch his grin widen. Laila moves forward to stand between me and Ace's desk, wiggling out of her bra. I hold my breath at the sight of her breasts. Her areolas can't be larger than a quarter, and her nipples are fully erect. Leaning forward, she runs the tip of her finger across my lower lip before reaching down to her panties.

I try to look away, I swear, but there's something keeping my eyes locked on the tiny triangle between her legs. More so, because she's keeping her legs closed as she drops her panties down. Okay, I admit, I'm getting turned on by a woman for the first time in my life and can even see myself spending a few minutes of passion with her. My heartbeats shoot up, and I'm most likely glowing red with the thoughts of having her in private only for me.

She hops on the edge of the desk, her knees still glued together, and elegantly moves her legs up and down. Ace keeps his annoying smile on his face, and his cock is still unmoved by Laila's dazzling moves.

My mouth plops open as she spreads her knees apart and places her feet on either side of my chair, revealing to me her smooth vagina in its full glory. Her clit is small, almost nonexistent, and the slit that separates the waxed lips of her sex is pink and glittering with moisture. I struggle to keep my hands from reaching over and touching her there.

I push back against my chair despite the urges inside me forcing me to do the opposite to get close to her. "Okay, I guess ... that's enough." I work hard to tear my eyes away from her sex to look up at her face. "You're beautiful in every way," I find myself saying to her and hear Ace burst into laughter.

"Okay, Laila, that's it for today. Thank you," Ace says. Laila flashes me a shy smile and collects her bra, panties, and dress before leaving the office.

Ace lifts both hands and points them down to his cock that is soft and tiny, as if he weren't present during Laila's hot performance. "She has absolutely no effect on me."

I wish I could say the same for myself. "It's

because you already fucked her."

Shaking his head, Ace crooks a finger at me. "Now, it's your turn. Take off that jacket and then the rest of your clothes."

I feel too hot inside my jacket anyway, so I stand, shake it off my shoulders, and toss it over my chair. His penis moves to my utter shock because what is watching me take off a jacket in comparison to Laila's completely naked body?

I smile and tug the hem of my shirt from my skirt and begin undoing the buttons. Ace shifts in his chair to get himself into a comfortable position, palms his hardening penis to rub it up and down, while his eyes are fixed on my body. My pulse quickens at the lust brewing in his beautiful eyes. My hands hasten their work, and soon I'm without a shirt. I might have overreacted to Laila's nakedness a little too much, but it's nothing compared to the desire shooting inside me at the sight of Ace teasing his penis in front of me.

When I push down my skirt and get out of it, Ace pushes his chair back and points at his desk. The sensual music is still on, and I take my steps in rhythm to the tune as I walk in my high heels and underwear toward his desk and then lower my rear end on its edge just enough to support myself as I spread my legs wide for him.

"Take them off," he orders, his eyes doing a quick scan of my body. I wonder if I looked as hypnotized as Ace does right now when Laila was dancing for me. Licking my lips, I reach for the clasp of my bra and pull it down, arching my chest up to push my small breasts up. Compared to Laila's large globes, I'm poorly endowed in that department, but Ace growls as if he's seen the most erotic sight of his life.

Taking courage in his eagerness and dangerously hard cock, I move my hands down to my panties and take them off as mysteriously as Laila did, keeping my knees glued together not to reveal any sight of my sex. However, Ace isn't as patient as I was with Laila and pushes my knees apart and stares at my sex like a starving man before a feast, before launching down to catch my most vulnerable part between his lips.

He cups my buttocks and pushes me against his face to better position his mouth between my legs as his tongue wanders through the slick of my sex from bottom to top. A shrill moan escapes me as his devious mouth begins to suck me with vigor, and I shudder as the desire spreads to each and every corner of my body. Wrapping my legs around his neck, I lean back on his desk, enjoying the first signals of a delicious rapture rolling from my core out.

He lifts his head to look at me. "You're soaking wet, baby. Did Laila turn you on?"

I can't respond to his inquisition without humiliating myself, but the heat on my face must have given him a satisfactory answer, because he's shaking his head teasingly and smiling.

"Talk to me." He forces his thumb against my clit to get the words out of me. "Did you want to suck her tits? Huh? Taste her down there?"

My hands cover my face without my control because Ace has a point. I haven't consciously thought of the things I could do with Laila, but she did turn me on.

"You know what would be so hot?" Ace continues with his mind games. "You two smashing your pussies together, scissoring each other."

"Shut up and go back to what you were doing." I fist my hands in his hair and gently guide him down, and he eagerly resumes his position and lets his tongue stir up more tingling emotions between my legs. Two large fingers push and knead the swollen flesh around my opening, teasing me slowly with their imminent invasion, and then slip forcefully inside me, inducing fireballs of arousal within my core. My body moves in rhythm to Ace's fingers and tongue. My moans get louder with each thrust.

Is it going to be this powerful every time he has his hands on me? Will I always lose my mind and completely surrender myself to him? Will there ever come a time where he will cease to render me thunderstruck?

I guess I know the answer to that one. The unforeseeable events of the upcoming weekend will likely put an end to the paradise of wild emotions I'm having in Ace's arms. I'll have my soul locked and my body numbed afterwards, like a rape victim, although nothing will be without my consent. In theory.

No! I shouldn't ruin the beauty of the present in fear of the distant future. I just need to enjoy the generosity given to me. Ace's ministrations are worth life itself. I would let him play with my sex for hours to come if I could, and that would be my paradise. His fingers pick up the speed, and I have no choice but to embrace the climax. My arms and legs go limp as I freeze.

"Let's take the party to the bed." Ace scoops me up and carries me to the room attached to his office, throwing me over to the bed where our love affair first started.

Hazed and breathing heavily, I watch him get rid of his slacks, boxers, and shirt, and lie next to me. "Are you too tired for me?"

"No way." I roll on my side to hug him. He lowers his head and kisses me. He's so sweet, so caring, his touches and kisses so cautious and soft, I can't help but be reminded of the men who are just the opposite of him. At that moment, all I can think of is the weekend ahead of me. What will the men be like? What will they do to me? It'll be an outrageous emotional trauma, but what will I do if they physically hurt me? To think of a stranger taking it against my will, makes me want to get a license and buy the biggest gun out there.

I draw back but keep my fingers on his cheek, working hard not to show my sadness. "I need you to do something for me."

"Anything."

"I want to try ... anal sex."

His face lights up with a full-tooth smile first, then tenses. "Why?"

I won't lie, but I won't share my fear with him either. "I can't tell you."

"If you don't, then I won't do it."

"You must be the first guy who has ever turned down an anal sex offer from a willing girl."

"I don't care." He drops his head on the pillow and keeps his eyes trained on me.

"Have you ever done it?"

He snorts out his yes. Of course he has. Why do I even bother to ask? "How many times?"

"Enough times to have lost count," he answers.

"Then you should be good at it."

"Well." He smirks and gives me a seductive once-over.

"Please. Let's do it." I can't believe I am begging for anal sex. And worse, he's turning me down.

"Tell me first why you want it."

He won't give in unless I confess. Shrugging, I move up on the bed and place my head on his chest, spreading my fingers on his six-pack. "I want to be prepared."

"For what?"

"For the weekend. If Michael's guests want to have anal sex with me..."

He jumps up on the bed with so much force that I slide down on my back. Fear fills my heart at the sight of the rage playing on his face, just like the day he came close to raping my ass. What's with him and his outbursts that make me shiver with fright?

He holds both of my hands gently and brings them up to his lips. "I'd rather burn down the whole building than let any man take advantage of you that way."

"How about Chloe? You'll risk her life if you attempt to do anything reckless."

His sudden anger soon is replaced with deep lines of misery at the mentioning of his sister. I don't know anything about his past or how much he had to go through in Michael's hands, but something tells me it's more than the physical pain Michael can inflict upon Chloe that's stressing him so. I want to save him from all the troubles. If my ass has to be put on the line to get his sister back, then that's what will have to be.

I reach up and touch the lines across his

forehead and between his furrowed brows. His gaze drops down on the bed, perhaps in shame of not having the power to protect the people he cares for. "We don't know what exactly will take place, but there's nothing wrong with being prepared for the worst."

"I won't let that happen."

He won't back down; that's why I need to try something else. A more feminine and a less confrontational method. What man can say no to a naked woman using her sweet and sexy voice for a favor? And all that before sex? For sex? He'll be a goner in my hands.

I give him a few minutes to cool down while biting my lower lip with intent and stealing seductive glances at his body. When he looks more or less his neutral self, I gently push his chest so he lies down on the bed and let my fingers wander slowly on his clearly defined chest and six-pack. His cock is deflated, but it's the easiest thing to take care of.

When for once I'd appreciate a man to follow his cock's desire, he has to follow his brain. Time has come to give the cock its power back. I slither down and position myself between his legs, all the while staring directly at his face, which is now looking back at me with suspicion.

"What are you doing?" he asks. One of those questions that deserves only a "What do I look like I'm doing?" for an answer.

I lower my head and place a kiss on the head of his cock. It's soft, as opposed to his firm body, and feels alien as if he's loaning it from someone else.

"Seducing me won't get you anywhere. I'm not fucking your ass."

We'll see about that. My hands are relaxed on his abs while my lips shower his cock and shaven balls with sweet kisses. I rub my cheek against the tender skin of his genitals and giggle when his cock stirs beneath my face and starts getting harder. The bigger it gets the more persuasive power I will have over Ace. When this is over, he'll be eating out of my hand and begging to get a taste of my ass.

I've never imagined giving a free pass to a man for my butt, but the thought of Ace pumping into me doggy style is nothing short of arousing.

His cock is now at its full length, glorious and menacing in equal parts. I open my mouth and take it in, but softly, sweetly, without any pressure.

For all I know, he can use my trick against me and come in my mouth within seconds if I suck him real hard.

"It's not going inside your ass," Ace murmurs but in reality he's trying to keep his conviction intact. Fool. Doesn't he know his conviction is only as strong as I want it to be?

I give his cock one long, slow suck and take it out of my mouth, letting my hand take over the teasing. "You know I'm virgin back there. Can you imagine how tight I must be, how firmly I'll wrap around your cock? Just like a glove."

He closes his eyes, perhaps to let his mind imagine my suggestion.

"Are you thinking of fucking me against the wall?" Really, I have no idea if it's a plausible position for anal sex, but that doesn't matter at this point because Ace seems to be getting into an irreversible 'I'm gonna fuck you hard' mood. "You'll go where no other man has been. You'll own me everywhere without any limitation."

"Lindsay, enough." He's breathing through his mouth, his hips moving in a leisurely speed to the rhythm of my hand around his member.

I lick his cock from base to top and move

down to suck his testicles. I admit having so much power over a man isn't just exciting but scary too. "You were right about one thing," I say using my seductive tone. "I got very turned on by Laila. We can call her in. I can lick her pussy while you fuck my ass. Wouldn't you love that?"

"Fuck, Lindsay."

"Yeah, baby. That's exactly what I want. I want you to fuck me in every possible way."

Slowly he opens his eyes and directs those topaz irises on me, taking my breath away with the lust darkening them. "You don't know what you're getting yourself into."

"I trust you and I love getting physical with you. I want to enjoy you in a way I've never enjoyed a man before." I lower my voice and say with the most innocent voice I can, "Is that too much to ask?" I bury my face into his genitals, plastering his cock against my lips.

Loud laughter shakes his body, and he runs his fingers through my hair, pushing my face further against his penis. "I thought JJ was a master manipulator. Now I see he doesn't have half the tactics you have."

"So ... are you going to test the uncharted

territories of my behind?"

"As much as I'd love that, I can't do it right now."

I raise my head to look up at him. "Why not?"

"You're not ready."

"I can be." If only I knew how, though...

"Let see. Get on all fours." He moves down the bed to stand beside it while I get on my knees and turn my back against him. He gently pushes my back down so I'm in doggy style in front of him.

My heart starts drumming hard, and my breathing gets shorter. I tilt my head to peek at him. As much as I want Ace to be the one to pop the cherry of my ass, I'd rather have no one touch me there. Special circumstances require special sacrifices. If my ass's virginity is what I'll have to sacrifice to get myself out of this hairy situation, then I shouldn't think twice about it.

Ace places both his hands on my butt cheeks, spreading them wide apart. His penis is poking menacingly. Honestly, how will that enormous thing enter my ass when I still have problems accepting its huge size into my vagina?

I close my eyes. My body goes taut at the thought of the damage I might incur back there. Tear, hemorrhoids, what if I can't sit normally ever again? Will my walking change? What if I lose control of my bowels? Seriously, how can anyone claim to love anal sex when so much is at risk?

"Relax," I hear Ace say then feel his lips on my skin. "I can't do it if you don't completely relax." Instead of following his suggestion, I jerk but only because he bites one of the cheeks and spanks the other one.

"Hey, I didn't ask for a spanking," I warn him loudly.

"That's part of the deal, baby. The two go hand in hand." His lips move between the cheeks slowly, teasingly.

I feel glad for having all the hair waxed in that area when he sticks out his tongue and starts licking my anus. His hands push the cheeks wide apart so his tongue has access to my virgin entrance. I must admit it's an odd feeling, but mostly because I have difficulty understanding how someone can enjoy licking someone else's ass. But, as the seconds pass, it starts to get into me and I wonder why I'd never even thought about letting any man try it before.

"You have the sweetest ass I've ever tasted, baby," he says between his licks, and I hope he's being honest. One of his hands moves down, and he thrusts two fingers inside my vagina, earning a soft moan out of me. He slides his other hand on my butt and starts massaging my anus before slipping a finger inside me. I yelp with pain and drop my head down on the bed, wrapping my arms around the pillow.

"I'm not fucking your ass tonight," he says. I'm not sure if I'm relieved or disappointed. If just one finger gives me so much pain, I can't imagine the amount his penis will cause. Despite his declaration, he keeps his fingers inside my vagina and anus while licking the surrounding area. One is painful, while the other one gives me a hell of a lot of pleasure. Soon the pleasure outweighs the pain, and I feel my anus relaxing. Taking advantage of the softness perhaps, Ace pushes his finger further inside until it can go no more and holds it still for a moment.

It's not painful anymore, but certainly uncomfortable, like being completely full. Not to mention the fact that his finger isn't in the most hygienic part of my body, although I showered after going number two. I should stop over-evaluating it and start enjoying it. After all, I too enjoy inserting my finger in a man's butt while being intimate. Why shouldn't Ace get at least some fun out of it? The fact that his penis is still hard should be enough proof of his pleasure despite the shit he's dealing with back there. Literally.

Pulling his fingers out of my vagina, he replaces them with his raging penis, and I almost pass out with the force of it because it feels double its usual size and makes me forget about the occupant in my ass.

"Now, baby, start talking," Ace says between his leisurely thrusts.

"Huh?"

"Tell me what you'd do with Laila."

"I can't."

"Why not?"

I moan to answer him. I'm too busy registering the explosions going on inside my sex to make up some hot fantasy for his liking, but when he stops moving and starts pulling out his cock, I have no recourse but to provide him with a juicy scene.

"I'd surprise her in her room and ... and fondle her breasts and kiss her lips."

He drives his cock back into me and stops again when he's deep inside. "Oh, yeah? Would you suck her nipples too?"

"Sure."

"What else?"

"If she's willing, good. But if not, I'd grab her by the hair and drag her on to her bed."

"Ahh. My girl. I know you would. Go on."

"I'd tie her up to the bed and slowly unbutton her dress."

He pulls his finger out of my butt and slowly pushes it back inside again. To my surprise, it doesn't hurt at all this time. Only it intensifies the feeling of his penis inside my sex. Are the two things somehow connected? I need an intensive anatomy lesson on that region.

"What if she screams?" Ace asks.

"She can scream all she wants. I'd get her all naked and..."

"And?"

""And I'd enjoy her."

"Fuck, give me details."

"I'd finger her vagina to get her horny, then I'd fuck her and myself with dildos."

"Fuck, that's hot. But I have a better suggestion. How about I fuck you with my cock instead of a dildo and you fuck her with whatever you want?" With that, he grabs my hip with his free hand and starts ramming into me at high speed while his finger in my butt follows the same rhythm of his cock. My hands can barely hold on to the bed sheets to keep me in place against his furious attack.

The vision of Ace fucking me while I work Laila up through her climax hits me as strongly as Ace's onslaught, and my own orgasm starts crashing through me. Ace slows down, letting me enjoy each and every wave, stroking my core, and then pulls his penis out.

Before I know what's going on, I feel him poking at my anus and sliding his penis inside it slowly and with relative ease, thanks to the natural lube of my vagina sheathing him. I scream with shock when he shoots his release inside my ass straight, without full penetration, and stay paralyzed for some time without daring to change position to keep the damage to a minimum as his penis pulses out his seed inside me.

"This is absolutely the sweetest ass I've ever fucked," Ace murmurs between his heavy breaths while cautiously sliding out of me. I'm too ashamed to look at him and see his dick coated with my shit because that sight surely has the power to gross me out and make me swear off anal sex altogether.

"You okay?" he asks softly and leaves a soft kiss on the small of my back.

"Yeah."

"I'll be back in a second." Smacking my ass cheek one last time, he heads to the bathroom. I drop down on my belly, hyper-aware of my butt and Ace's spunk gushing out of it as I listen to the sound of the shower next door. It is not half as traumatic as I imaged it to be, only a little too tender to touch. And I'm glad it was a man as gentle and arousing as Ace who initiated it.

Ace comes out of the shower with a towel wrapped around his tight hips and sets about cleaning my butt with wet wipes, brushing my back with loving kisses and soft strokes every now and then. I come close to crying with the affection he's showering me with. Whatever grudge Michael might have against me, he also made it possible for me to meet a gem of a man. And just for that, I don't wish for Michael's death.

When Ace is done cleaning me, I pull him beside me under the sheets and embrace his body tightly.

Having him close infuses sweet and warm emotions into my heart, like the ones I feel for Taylor. If something were to happen to her, I'd never be the same person again, and I'm afraid Ace is becoming the next person after Taylor who has that significance in my heart.

"Just to make it clear, I would never attempt to force Laila or any other human being to have sex. I just told you that fantasy to tease you. Nothing further. Okay?"

He simply smiles at my remark and closes his eyes, shielding his face with his arm.

"What? Are you going to sleep now? Where's my after-sex clingy moment?" I frown at him, but he's quickly drifting into sleep. His arm around my shoulder gets heavy; his legs jerk, and within seconds, his breathing evens out.

First he complains that I attempt to leave him right after sex, but now that I want to stay with him to cuddle, he's completely ignoring my need to talk out my first anal experience with an insensitively timed nap. Why do I even get upset, though? He's a man. Being a jerk is a part of who they are; it's engraved into their DNA.

My head moves up and down with the rhythm of his chest. Well, at least he doesn't snore. I follow the curves of his pecs and abs with the tip of my index finger to keep myself from shooting myself out of the sheer boredom while waiting for him to wake up.

I try not to think about my back, but the harder I try, the sorer it feels there. They must have some soothing balm or lotion somewhere here for cases like mine. However, I'll have to wait for Ace to wake up because I neither have the nerve to ask around for lotion for my ass, nor the strength to get to my feet.

"Don't touch me," Ace murmurs and I instantly go on high alert, watching his face. "Get your hands off of me," he continues with his low mumbles. I wonder for the briefest second whether he's ordering me to leave him alone, but no. His eyes are still closed, and he's rolling his head left and right as if in a dream.

"Ace, darling. Wake up." I reach up to cup his

chin, but he yanks my hand away and shoves me onto the bed. I fall on my butt and immediately cringe with the burn stinging at my anus.

"Let me go...arghhh, it hurts... Let me go."

"Oh, God. Ace. What's going on? Wake up. You're scaring me." Ignoring my pain, I grab his shoulder and shake him, yelling his name at his ear. When he finally wakes up, there are tears in his reddened eyes, and he's sobbing loudly.

"What ... What's going on?" he asks, breathing heavily. His eyes skim around with an empty look in them then land on me blankly, as if he doesn't recognize me.

"Are you okay? I guess you were having a bad dream." I hesitate to lift my hand to dry his tears for fear of being yanked away again, but I do it anyway, and wipe his cheeks with my fingers.

"I think so." He pushes up and places his feet on the ground, but I move up, despite the burn in my butt, and wrap my arms around his waist to keep him still.

"Tell me what you were dreaming about?"

"Nothing important. Some age-old dream."

"I want to hear it."

His breaths are the only sound in the room while I wait for his answer.

"Please."

He shakes his head, grips my hands to free himself from my hold, and stands. Not looking at me, he rushes to the bathroom, and I'm left to listen to the minimal sounds he's making behind the closed door to guess what he's up to. When I hear more sobs, I move down, cautiously though because my butt is burning more with each move, and grab his shirt from the floor, putting it on before walking to the bathroom.

Thankfully, the bathroom door isn't locked, and I sneak inside to see what's going on. Ace is collapsed on the sink, his head hidden under his arm, and crying. My heart goes numb at the sight of him in so much pain. But for what, I've yet to find out.

"Ace, love. Talk to me. What's going on?" I take a cautious step toward him, holding my breath.

He rises up, his face haunted, hurting, and glances at me through the mirror. "I am... I don't know." He presses his lips into a thin line as soon as words are out of his mouth.

"Tell me about the dream you had."

"I don't remember the details. I just remember being suffocated."

That doesn't sound good. "Do you have it often?"

"Not really. Only a few times... If I think about it, it started again since you entered my life."

"Me? What does it have to do with me? I've never tried to strangle you or anything."

He shrugs with a painful smile on his lips.

I replay his sentence in my mind. "What do you mean it started again? Did you have it before?"

"I'm not sure. It feels like I did."

My curiosity is piqued. "What do you think triggered it?"

"Will you please stop analyzing me? It's just a silly dream."

"Hey. I'm trying to be helpful. You don't need to be an ass about it," I snap.

He turns around, his expression softening, and wraps his hands around my waist. "I'm sorry. It came out the wrong way. I just don't want to ruin our special moment.

"What special moment?" I stop to think what he means, and the burn in my butt comes to my rescue to remind me of that special moment. "Oh, that. You ruined it by falling asleep, silly," I joke and ruffle his hair playfully.

"Sorry, baby. I haven't gotten a good night's sleep since Chloe's kidnapping."

"Okay, you're forgiven."

His arms around my shoulders, we walk back to the room and he sets about putting on his boxers and slacks. He sees his shirt on me and opens an in-wall closet to get a clean white shirt for himself.

I remain standing while watching him get ready. "So, we never talked about how Michael was as a father."

"You'll not let it go, will you?"

When I shake my head no, he lets out an exasperated breath and starts, "He wasn't a father to us to begin with because he wasn't around most of the time, and when he was around, he treated us poorly. I mean really poorly, the worst way you can imagine."

"Did he abuse you physically?"

"You mean did he beat me up? Yes, he did. Over and over again, making the entire family watch while he beat the crap out of me, Zane, and Chloe. He's got severe anger issues and hurt us in the worst ways a father can hurt his child."

My mouth goes dry; my stomach churns at the thought of a defenseless child abused by an adult who is supposed to be his parent, his protector. My aunt and uncle might not have shown me and my sister the love they showed their biological children, but they'd never lifted a hand to us, either. I wish I had a chance to physically hurt Michael, although it won't fix all the damage he caused and is still doing to his children.

"Was your dream about him?" I ask.

"No. I don't know actually. I don't remember any details. Just the feeling of being suffocated."

Still, it's very likely that Ace dreamed about a past, long-forgotten horror with Michael.

"Chloe had it the worst though," Ace continues. "Michael has this sick idea of keeping Chloe's virginity intact. Because of that, no boy in high school could approach her, and if one was brave enough to, Chloe would be the one to pay. Every time Michael heard about some boy talking to Chloe, he'd strip her down and beat her in front of us."

"Jesus. You can't be serious. That's insane." I feel tears stinging my eyes.

"He did the same thing to her on Saturday night in front of Dylan. That's why I thought it'd be a good idea to hide Chloe from Michael at one of my friends' home. But now both of them are gone."

"We need to stop him. I don't know how we'll do it, but this has to come to an end." I run and throw myself to Ace's arms, hugging him tightly, caressing his back, hoping at least I can protect him from Michael's future harms, but also marveling at how Ace has come out so strong, yet gentle, and loving after surviving all that hatred and abuse.

The Investigation

I stay at Ace's place for the rest of the week, and to my surprise, neither Michael, nor any of his employees, particularly Edrick, has tried to put an end to my affair with Ace. I guess Michael has realized he has more power over me through Ace than without him.

Although my first anal sex experience was gentler than I'd ever imagined—no anal fissure or problems with sitting—I didn't initiate another round, and Ace never asked for it. I'm of the opinion that my ass needs a few months to recover from the shock of the one and only thrust of Ace's penis. However, I have no idea what I'll do if I'm forced into anal sex on the weekend by Michael's guests. I should seriously start considering the option of drugging anyone who lays eyes on my butt, if I want to keep my organs intact.

Instead of anal sex, Ace and I fill our free time making sweet love to each other. I watch him and am thrilled how he comes out of his shell, alive and resilient, when his lips find my lips and my body.

My colleagues wisely choose to ignore me, so does Julie by not responding to my menacing email. It can however hint to something else, a more dangerous plan to get back at me for my little threat in my email. The longer I ponder it, the more I get convinced some secret plan is brewing in her small head. More so when all she does when she sees me is politely smile. Just perfect. All I needed was one more person to deal with.

On Thursday morning, I convince Adam to give me a tour at the construction site of Michael's residential project he and Taylor are working on to rule out the possibility that the reason behind my recruitment might have something to do with it. The property is a huge, hundred-acre breathtaking beauty surrendered by tall oak trees. I can understand Dylan's bitterness about losing the land to Michael. Perhaps his relationship with Chloe isn't purely love-based, but rooted in the motivation to get his land back.

"Are you still dating Michael?" Adam asks and slams the car door.

"Actually no, but it's confidential. So, don't go around talking about it, okay?" I follow him into the construction area while examining the semi-finished buildings, some three-story, others single homes. "How much do you think the starting price for the condos will be?" Buying a home here looks like a good investment, considering the close distance to the city and the vast green area surrendering the homes.

"My estimation for the lowest priced two-bedroom would be in the one and one and a half million range."

My mouth hangs open. "That much?" That's most of the money I'll be getting from Michael's contract. That is, if I can get it at the end.

"Yeah, sure. The schools nearby have great

ratings. I-5 is only a five-minute drive away. Plus, Michael is having a shopping mall built on the north end of the territory, which should also attract buyers and investors."

"How much is Michael going to make if he can sell off everything?"

"There're sixty two-bedroom condos and another sixty three-bedrooms. He can easily make two-hundred million with those. The single homes should sell for at least five-million dollars. So that's another hundred million."

"What the... Seriously? That's a lot of money."

"That's not including the money he'll make from the mall. If he's not already a billionaire, he'll cross that border by the time he's done."

Zane's words echo in my mind. "He must have something else in mind to hire you, and I'm sure it's not related to your fame. He doesn't spend a penny without making sure he'll get at least three times more. If he's paying you the amount I have in mind, you can bet your ass he has no simple intentions, like covering up his homosexuality."

This must be it. Why he hired me to be his girlfriend must be somehow related to this land.

"Did you encounter any issues connected to the Macey Williams video?" I ask. "Did the video in any way affect the project or the home sales?"

Adam glances down at me with a curious expression. "No, not at all. If anything, it drew attention to the project. I heard about twenty percent more condos were sold within the three-month time frame right after the release of the video. Why do you ask?"

"Just curious."

Adam goes on showing me the buildings, giving me details about the building materials Michael demanded them to use for construction and the architectural and eco-friendly features of the edifices. Solar panels, the type of windows and window frames used, the style of roofing to boost conductive heat regulation ... With each explanation Adam gives, I feel less and less inclined to think this project is Michael's unusual reason for hiring me, because all in all, the project is a pioneering event in terms of energy efficiency and the top quality products used in it. In fact, I begin contemplating investing into a condo in the community before everything is snatched up. Not only will Michael profit from it, but also Taylor and Adam if the project finalizes with success.

On the other hand, if it's not this project or the land, then what is it that keeps me captive in Michael's hands? It's not like he's in love with Adam and using me to get to him. He has his lover somewhere, and from what I've heard, he's deeply in love with him. Besides, Adam had nothing to do with the Iron Slap video. It was Taylor, Macey Williams, me and the two other victims. Only women. Nothing a homosexual man would pay any attention to, if his intentions were only sexual in nature.

After the sightseeing, Adam and I join Taylor for dinner. Taylor mentions a new position opening up in their accounting department, hinting that I should apply for it. If I'd taken a job from her in the first place instead of going to Michael, none of this would have happened. I'm not completely sure if it'd have been better though. If this mystery is somehow, even remotely related to Taylor, it's a good thing that I'm in the middle of the action so I have a chance to protect her.

She's the closest person to me. If something were to happen to her, particularly because of me, I'd never forgive myself. The same way Ace must feel for not being able to protect his own sister? But, he's not showing any of the horror he must be feeling deep down to me. Perhaps, he learned to conceal his emotions throughout the abusive years.

Yet another day passes without me getting any closer to finding out Michael's secret intentions for me. So far, only the meeting with Tiffany Jordan helped. Actually, her revelation caused me even more confusion, but it's helped to some degree nevertheless. At least it desensitized me to the content of the video after having watched it over fifty times to figure out why Michael wanted to keep it a secret.

On Friday, I arrive at work a little earlier than usual to take advantage of having no one in the office to wrap up the project I've been working on. I have no way of knowing what I'll be doing after the weekend and don't want to let down the other team members who've worked their asses off to complete it before the deadline. I might not like my teammates personally, but they don't deserve to fail because of me.

Not to mention how much I love working on this project as it was the reason to give up on the warm space on the bed beside Ace and expose myself to L.A.'s morning chill to come to work. I was created to crunch numbers and give meaning to them. Why can't I just enjoy working hard on computations, making graphs, and drafting reports but instead have to dedicate my attention to intrigues and mysteries?

As if it's ordered from Michael himself, the other employees seem to be all focused and meticulous about the project today, much to my relief. And, I wind up completing my part by lunchtime. With the plan to devote my afternoon to the rest of the project in my mind, I collect my purse and jacket and head out for a quick lunch.

Edrick, however, has other plans for my afternoon, and my lunch break for that matter, and hauls me out for shopping for dresses and evening gowns I should be wearing for the weekend. After the shopping, he drives me to Pleasure Extraordinaire, per Michael's order, to check if the preparations taking place there are glamorous and elegant enough to honor Michael's guests. In other words, if the call girls are sexy and willing and if the alcohol is abundant.

Ace and I avoid showing any affection to each other in Edrick's presence, although I'm sure he's aware of our relationship.

Ace usually has only two other girls besides Laila in Pleasure Extraordinaire for clients who enjoy a company of a girl or just want to try it. However, for the party, he hired twenty new girls from a high-class agency that caters to men.

I wasn't aware that many girls would be called for or if they'll all get a chance to show their talents, considering the small size of the group who'll attend the party. A part of me whispers to myself that it's an attempt on Ace's part to divert attention from me to the new girls, but I can't help feeling protective about them. They are very young to begin with, their ages ranging between eighteen and twenty-one and they must be in this business for reasons other than simply enjoying serving perverted men's sexual desires. Money must be the main reason, or perhaps they're forced into it.

Ace looks cold and distant too as he walks Edrick and me through the suites where the party will be held and the guests who will accommodate in. All this preparation and money spent must mean something in Michael's book. Also, my presence beside him as his girlfriend.

Edrick picks out the dress I should wear at the welcome reception. It's a vine-red, knee-length dress with long sleeves. More on the conservative side than I'd have imagined. Though I'm not complaining about the choice of my dress, the outfits Edrick hands the girls to put on are outrageous. All two-piece, transparent lingerie that will leave nothing to the imagination.

JJ, Nick, and two other male escorts I haven't met before are expected to join the reception, but only as a partner to the girls in a dance show. I assume there won't be any ladies among Michael's guests, but I faintly remember the wife of the Minister of Internal Affairs will accompany her husband for the trip. Goes to show how much the Minister cares about his wife's entertainment.

When Edrick deems everything is set for the weekend, he advises me to get at least nine hours of sleep in case the reception tomorrow night lasts till dusk. It sounds more like an order though, but I'm happy to oblige orders that are for my own good.

Ace sends one of the young boys to escort Edrick out and closes his office door behind him, leaning against it. He looks helpless like an animal doing the walk of death to the slaughterhouse.

"I don't want those girls being abused by Michael's people," I say and slip my arms around his waist, resting my head on his chest.

"Neither do I. I hope it won't come to that,

but it's probably wishful thinking." He digs his nose into my hair and sniffs deeply.

I feel physical pain at the thought of the girls, especially Clarice, one of the two virgins on the girls' team, being forced to comply with a bunch of pigs' sexual desires. She claims to be twenty, but the innocence on her face and the fear in her eyes tell me she can't be older than sixteen, maximum seventeen. Jesus, how did she end up working as an escort? Since she's also the prettiest among the girls, I have no doubt she'll be requested as the first. I would seriously prefer having all the guests perform anal sex on me than having Clarice go through the terror of her life by losing her virginity in a demeaning and painful way.

The girls, Chloe, Ace's business, me... So much is at stake for a handful of greedy perverts. The next days will make or break us all.

The Evening

I spend the Friday night at Taylor's home. We order take-out food and watch the last episodes of Frat House, feeling grateful to the producers for coming up with such a great show that can pull out laugh after laugh from me during one of the grimmest times of my life. When I pop the news to Taylor about the possibility of the show being canceled, she groans loudly as if in pain, while Adam voices his full agreement with the decision. It's beyond my grasp how someone can't enjoy the story of four hunky college guys running after sexy co-eds for one-night stands. Oh, wait. Now I see how.

On Saturday morning, I wake before dawn and stay in the bed Taylor assigned to me, contemplating the hours ahead. Finally, I decide I can't control whatever will happen to me but what I do with it is all up to me. I can choose to allow the horrible events to drag me down or accept them as part of life and be grateful for not facing challenges worse than this.

It's not like Taylor is fighting against cancer and living her final days—now that has the power to change me fully for the worst, but not a bunch of sex-crazed men. There are families who lose their fathers to war or parents who bury their dead babies. Taylor and Adam have been yearning to have children for so long and lost their baby during stillbirth. However, they didn't let it destroy their lives but came out of it stronger than ever. What's being forced to have sex with a few men in comparison to that kind of pain? I'll be doing it to protect someone.

And besides, why should I give any man more importance than he deserves? If I let those filthy men hurt me, I'll be doing exactly that. If anything, they should worry that the events upcoming might be used against them. If not today, very likely in the future.

With that conviction, I get up, start my day with a long, hot shower, and have a light breakfast with Taylor and Adam.

As the hours pass, however, I can't help the fear creeping back into my heart. Each time I feel like I'll faint with anxiety, I repeat to myself that this will soon pass.

I change into the vine-red gown Edrick chose for me, but ignore the Louboutins and go for my humble but comfortable flats when I remember reading about the quality of shoes being one of the most important determining factors for several concentration camp survivors. I'll not have even a tenth of the difficulties those people had to face in the hands of Nazis, but there's no disadvantage to putting on a pair of comfortable shoes in case things get heated up, and I might need my fight or flight instincts to survive.

At five p.m., Ace receives a text from Edrick about the guests' upcoming arrival in fifteen minutes. Ace hurries to take a last-minute assessment of the suite the reception party will be held in while I walk to the entrance with the girls, Nick, and JJ.

My heart is beating so hard while waiting for the door to be opened I can feel the drumming in my mouth. I don't know if JJ has the slightest idea about what is awaiting me, but he gives me warm, encouraging smiles each time our eyes meet. Laila is standing by him, both across from me, and I can tell by her hand fidgeting that she doesn't feel comfortable either. The girls are wearing the silk red robes Edrick picked up for them together with several-inches-high heels.

Ace finally shows up and opens the front door. We watch two stretch limousines and three black SUVs park in the garden. First the bodyguards in the SUVs leave, and as soon as they're done scanning the surroundings, one hurries to open the door of one of the limousines. A blonde woman, possibly in her early forties, gets out first, glancing around behind her sunglasses. She heads directly for the stairs without caring about the people back in the limousine or the bodyguards. Her tall, delicate figure beneath her army-green skirt suit moves fluently with each step, fearless as if she's going to her own house.

A man, also tall but with light-brown hair,

catches my attention. He climbs out of the limousine like a celebrity, straightens his black jacket, and takes his time while talking to the bodyguard who opened to the door.

Michael is the next one to leave the limousine. I draw in a sharp breath at the sight of him, re-living the last minutes in his office as if they happened just now. His face is all friendly smiles as he listens to the bodyguard talk with the other man, then points toward the front door with his hand so both men move up the stairs. Two other men follow them, but I can't tell if they're bodyguards or part of the guest group.

I'm momentarily distracted by Ace as he welcomes the blonde woman, shaking her hand, guiding her inside. When Michael arrives, he heads directly toward me. I have no idea how he expects me to behave in front of his guests. Shall I kiss him on the lips like the two lovers that we're posing to be or just give him a quick hug? He stares at me blankly as opposed to my gaze that's full of questions.

Where's Chloe? Did you hurt her? Will you let her go tonight? Will you set me free?

He leans down, kisses my cheek quickly, and takes my hand in his while he introduces each of the guests. I work very hard not to yank his hand away from mine and find the solution in concentrating on the new faces.

Demyan and Devora Vasilyev; the Minister of Interior Affairs and his wife. The two men who arrived last are the minister's two brothers, Vas and Pavlo Vasilyev. I can't make any specific assumption regarding the age of the two brothers, but they can't be younger than thirty or older than forty-five. Both with dark-brown hair, they wear expensive-looking navy-blue suits as if they're here for a business meeting or a political discussion, not to flirt around with call girls.

I don't miss the appreciative look on Devora's face despite the glasses covering up her eyes as she shakes hands with Ace. While Demyan Vasilyev only acknowledges Ace, Vas and Pavlo go through the entire two lines to introduce themselves and ask the names of the girls and how they are. I try not to think of their attention as malicious, but the way they're eyeing some of the girls, especially Vas, gives me shivers.

Although Michael introduces me to Demyan as his girlfriend, he only nods at me, without caring to utter a word of acknowledgement to me. In normal situations, I'd take his attitude for rude, but now I'm content with being ignored. I hope he continues his uncaring attitude toward me and the girls too.

Only Devora speaks English without an accent, and I wonder if she lived in the States as a child. She also completely ignores the girls, while even Demyan doesn't hesitate from taking careful looks at some of them. Not in a jealous wife way, though, but as if we're invisible.

With Devora and Ace in the front, Michael, Demyan, and I behind them, we walk to the suite for the reception. Michael's grip around mine is tight and possessive. I try to take long strides trying to match his speed. Vas and Pavlo have already started their entertainment program on the way to the suite, because they begin laughing and joking with the two of the older girls behind us, while speaking Russian to each other in between.

I dare take a look back and see Clarice between Laila and JJ, looking pale and worried. If no man touches her and she keeps her innocence intact throughout the weekend, I'll consider it as a success.

As soon as we enter the suite, a group of four musicians starts with a romantic tune, and I realize I didn't pay enough attention to the effort Ace put into the preparations of the party all this time because of my stress. The suite is large enough to host fifty guests easily. The lights are dim, almost orange in tint. A huge oval table with ten chairs around sits close to the door with six additional tables of four spread around the large room for guests who may prefer to have some privacy. Red loveseats and leather armchairs look inviting right before the stage.

And, the smell. Oh the smell. Ace either discovered the most enticing floral room fragrance or paid someone lots of money to dilute an expensive female perfume, because it smells heavenly fresh and sweet.

The décor, the music, the smell. Nothing is overwhelming to the senses, everything is in perfect harmony.

Four girls move toward the stage, shrugging out of their robes on the way to display their flawless bodies beneath their skimpy pieces of clothing, and take their places together with JJ and Nick before the musicians for their dance performance.

A server hastens to collect their tossed robes from the floor and disappears behind the stage. As if on cue, the rest of the girls start spreading around in different directions at the same time and stroll leisurely, I guess, to lure their clients into some action. With that sickening sight, the magic of the suite comes crashing down in my eyes. No amount of classy décor can take away the cheapness of having girls walk around almost fully naked, up for grabs by the men.

Michael lets go of my hand and takes his place on one of the red leather armchairs at the center of the sofa set. Demyan, Vas, and Pavlo follow suit and sit in the chairs around him. Ace pulls out cigars for them and signals the servers to bring out the liquor.

I remain standing still, close to the entrance, not knowing if I should join the men or the girls who are now walking around aimlessly. If Michael wanted me beside him, he'd have made his wish clear, and if he's not calling me at the moment, then I shouldn't disturb him.

As I start to move toward Clarice, who's watching the dance show with a chaste smile on her face, Devora calls me by my name. "Lindsay, isn't it? Your name is Lindsay."

I spin on my heels abruptly in the direction Devora's commanding voice is coming from. "Yes, ma'am," I find myself saying.

Devora smiles, casually sizing me up. I realize her eyes are light green and beautiful, adding a friendly tone to her otherwise stern face. "Lindsay Doheny. I thought your name was familiar. Now I know why. You're Taylor Garnett's sister."

"That's right." I bite my lip quickly not to spill out another embarrassing 'ma'am'. "Have you met my sister?" I ask, although the odds of Taylor meeting the wife of a Russian diplomat and not telling me are close to zero.

"No." She shakes her head, narrowing her eyes as if contemplating what or how much she should share with me. "But, I have heard a lot about her."

"She's the CEO of Edelman Construction that runs a project Michael has in northern Los Angeles," I add nonchalantly to prompt her to spill out what she might know about Taylor.

"I know."

"I hear most of the condos are already under contract or already sold."

Her smile widens, and her eyes leave mine to find Michael in the group ahead of us. "You don't need to give me any information about the project. I know every detail about it, perhaps even more than Michael knows."

"Oh."

She returns her gaze to me, searching my face inquisitively. "Your sister has an admirable career. But what I don't understand is why you chose to pose as a girlfriend to Michael? Is it the money?"

Her words have the effect of a cold shower on me. Being compared to my sister in such a bad light when all I was trying to achieve was to set my career straight hurts more than I expected.

"Yes. I needed money," I admit without going into details of the miserable job-hunting period I had.

A waitress offers us champagne. After a few seconds of trying to decide if I have the luxury to allow my mind a little light-headedness, I mirror Devora and take a glass for myself.

"You poor little thing. You came in for the money, now you can't get out even if you try," Devora says in a teasing tone.

"How do you know?"

"You should know everything about the person you're doing business with. That's rule number one when going into deals worth hundreds of millions of dollars. In your case, if you can manage to keep your mouth shut, you should be able to save your little ass after the project is over."

"Which project are you talking about?" I ask, curious to see if it's the construction project she's hinting at."

"Oops. Have I said too much? Like I suggested, keep your mouth shut!" She lifts her finger to place it on her lips, motioning for me to keep quiet and then grabs another glass of alcohol.

Shit. I knew my recruitment had something to do with the construction project. Now I have to find a way to figure out the real connection between the two incidents. I scan around the suite in an attempt to hide my thoughts from Devora and realize Ace is glancing at me while I sip from my drink. His expression is pained yet filled with tenderness and longing, and I wish I could go hug him and steal a lustful kiss from his parted lips.

"Oh, I see money isn't the only thing you get out of your arrangement with Michael," Devora says, catching me off-guard as I stare at Ace. "He's adorable in every sense. Not pretentious or a narcissist like most American men are, but a thoroughly handsome guy who behaves as if his looks are nothing special to brag about. I almost think he's Russian. He has that wild masculinity about him that our men have."

I tear my gaze away from Ace to look up at Devora and see her grinning devilishly. How could she guess Ace has Russian blood?

"Is he as good in bed as his looks?" she asks.

"Just like you suggested a second ago, I'm not allowed to talk about anything regarding Michael, including his family members. I assume you'll understand, considering the secrecy of your own visit to the States."

"Smart girl, but our visit here is no more secret than Michael wants it to be. We don't care if the FBI finds out why we are here. It's only Michael and his irrational fears."

It reminds me of another irrational fear he has: people finding out about his homosexuality. Looks like that's not the only thing that's eating at him. "Does that mean you're free to share it with me?"

"Of course it does, but I won't. Why would I

trust an American girl? It'd be as illogical as the Russian government giving up on nuclear weapons or accepting the USA to rule the UN. However, I will tell you this much." She moves closer to me and leans down, still staring at my face with her devilish smile. "We're not here for a friendly chat or sightseeing. We're here to take back what the US took from us: Afghanistan, Ukraine, the entire Russian Empire."

What the hell is she talking about? I'd rather have keeping my ass safe as the main problem for the weekend than trying to escape from an international war zone. And when did Russia ever have control over Afghanistan? I guess I should waste less time on sex and read more about history.

Then, out of the blue, she bursts into laughter, pointing her finger at me. "You should see your face. That's hilarious. Did you seriously believe me? You, silly thing. We're here for only business. To make money, then off we go and you can have your boyfriend all to yourself."

What can I say? She got me good. I honestly thought I should find a way to sneak out and contact the FBI to inform them about the wicked plans of the Russian couple.

"Now it's your turn to answer. Is he good in bed?" she asks, while I try to find my tongue.

"I'm not in the position to answer that."

She studies my face for long enough to be considered rude, then crosses her arms over her chest, still holding her glass of champagne in one hand. "If you don't give me a clear answer, I'll take it as a green light to go ahead and try my chances with him."

Oh, the nerve she has to threaten me like that. She licks her lower lip in a slow, provocative way, and a disgusting image of her licking Ace's penis forms in my mind. I guess that's exactly what she wants me to envision and it is working. Yuck. I start thinking making me uncomfortable is more of her intention than trying out what Ace has to offer in bed. As long as she doesn't realize her threat, I'm fine with any kind of disturbing image occupying my mind.

"Do you seriously think the answer can in any way be a no?" I respond, reflecting the cynical tone she's used talking to me.

She laughs again, gulps down the entire glass of champagne, and orders more. I'm glad I can entertain at least one guest without losing my dignity.

"Looks like you and I are going to get along well. Here's the deal. You'll find a way to distract my husband and I'll have a little fun."

Exactly the thing I've been trying to avoid all this time—well, just the distracting the minister part, because I don't care if she sleeps with all the Pleasure Extraordinaire escorts.

The dance show ends, and JJ and Nick walk the girls down the stage. The music changes to a modern interpretation of a classical song.

"Don't worry, I won't make a move on your boyfriend," Devora says. "I guess I can find a more giving one than your boyfriend."

If only she knew...

I follow the direction her eyes are fixed at and find her exchanging heated looks with JJ. How fitting. JJ will turn her life upside down in terms of sex and pleasure, but I guess she deserves it for playing with me like a toy.

Hoping she's the jealous type, I can't stop myself from asking, "How exactly am I supposed to distract Mr. Vasilyev?"

"I don't care how you do it, but just make

sure he doesn't go around looking for me for half an hour." She winks at JJ, who is sitting at a table a few feet away from us with his dance partners, and flaunts her hips as she walks toward the group of men.

I watch her intently as she joins the conversation with them for five minutes and then excuses herself, likely for the restroom. On her way out, she glances at JJ, points her chin toward the door and disappears with elegance and confidence oozing from her body. JJ gets her sign, but cleverly takes Clarice along with him as he leaves five minutes after Devora's departure.

"I can do it," I whisper to myself. There're only four guests, with Michael, five. Five might be an odd number but it isn't a number as destructive as seven. Besides, Ace is here.

I guess Michael has sensed Devora's plans, because he signals me to come to him with his finger, and Ace pulls a chair for me next to Michael's majestic seat. I take in a sharp breath of air that doesn't smell so sweet anymore with the fear rippling in me as Demyan's eyes now follow me attentively.

From the corner of my eye, I see Vas sitting at a table with Laila, and Pavlo is dancing with one of the dancers earlier in the show.

"What happened with your previous girlfriend? What was her name? Miss Tiffany Jordan," Demyan asks Michael the second my buttocks touch the chair. "She was a fine lady."

"Oh, yes, she was," Michael confirms Demyan's observation of Tiffany. "We had to split up due to unexpected events, but I can't complain because I got to meet this beautiful lady." Michael reaches over, smiling, to grab my hand and lifts it up to his lips. Bile rises in my throat, and I swallow hard not to throw up at the kiss of his lips on my knuckles. How could I ever have found him attractive? He's the very definition of repulsive with his pretentiousness, selfishness, and evilness.

"I've always admired your taste in women," Demyan says, scanning my body up and down, instantly adding himself to my list of disgusting men, thanks to the gleeful grin attached to his lips.

"Would you like to have dinner now?" Ace chimes in, saving me from Demyan's hungry stare.

"Dinner?" Demyan raises his hands up, palms facing the ceiling. "No. We don't have time for it. We should be going to the project. Shouldn't we? Michael."

The project. Will I accompany them during their ride to the project? Heavens, please!

Michael answers him. "We'll take a bit longer. There's someone I'd like you to meet."

For some reason, I immediately think of Clarice. Is Michael going to offer her to Demyan as a gift for their partnership? My chest constricts in pain with the revolting thoughts of Demyan taking Clarice's virginity here, in front of everyone.

Demyan looks around with a curious expression plastered on his red face, as if to say, "Who?"

"Let's skip the dinner and have only hors d'oeuvres for now." Michael glances at Ace, and just like that, Ace gets his message and calls a server to whisper in her ear the orders.

As we're served our hors d'oeuvres, a man with a strikingly familiar face appears at the doorway, and all the heads turn to him, as if someone has announced his arrival through loud speakers. The musicians stop, so do the murmurs in the suite.

The new guest is as tall as Michael, perhaps even taller, has clean-cut jet-black short hair, prominent blue eyes, and a strong jaw emphasizing his pouting lips. Casually dressed in a gray suit, he strides through the room toward us with authority.

With each step he comes closer to us, my memory yells at me that I know this guy, but how and where? Did I see him at Hawkins Media Group headquarters? At Taylor's company? Or perhaps on TV?

The feeling of familiarity becomes unbearable as he stops before us and runs his eyes on each of us intently, as if he's trying to hypnotize us into complying with his wishes.

Ace stands next to me, his hand touching the small of my back, and I feel an aura of protectiveness spreading from him over to me. Both Vas and Pavlo drop the girls and join us in our little union.

"Demyan," Michael is the first one to break the silence, "I suppose you've heard of Edward Neuberger, Attorney General of California."

Oh, that's how I know him. From the news. I guess I'm not as much of an idiot as Devora made me out to be. The Attorney General himself is gracing us with his presence in a party organized by Michael for Russian diplomats. Never in a million years would I have thought of finding myself surrounded by so many mighty men.

He's not only Attorney General but also running for the next gubernatorial election. I've been thinking about voting for another candidate, and now I remember why. Edward Neuberger gives me the impression of a cruel man, a Machiavellian-type personality. That cold expression seems to be permanent on his face, the smile never reaching his eyes. Just like how Michael is in reality but manages to hide it beneath his fake smiles and friendly demeanor. Perhaps this man is a warm-hearted man deep down beneath the harshness of his appearance.

"Of course I do." Demyan offers his hand in a practiced manner, introducing himself and his two brothers. "Good luck for the upcoming elections, but I guess you won't be needing any since everyone is saying you'll win."

Edward thanks Demyan for his observation and turns his gaze to Ace. For a brief second, I see a jolt in Edward's unfriendly eyes as he shakes hands with Ace, then he resumes his trained expression as Michael presents me to him.

Edward is the sixth guest in the party. Six is my favorite number of all time. It has never failed me. Which means Edward can't be dangerous or criminal. With that realization, I find my body relaxing a bit.

Despite Demyan's tactful protests against having dinner, we gather around the large table for dinner upon Edward's request. For some reason, Michael offers the main chair at the head of the table to Edward and sits beside him and across from Demyan. That's odd for many reasons, for one: Michael severely suffers from the Entitlement Personality Disorder and would never willingly let someone take his place as the head of any group he is in. Giving up on the main chair must be like a king giving up on his throne. And for the other, Demyan deserves that seat for being the guest who's coming from overseas, not to mention his diplomatic ranking as the Minister of Interior Affairs of Russia as opposed to Edward's status as Attorney General of California.

I sit between Michael and Ace, slightly amused by the fact that one is the angel and the other is the devil.

To add more mystery, all the girls leave the suite while servers place our plates on the table. Is the sight of the girls suddenly not appetizing enough for their majesties? Or perhaps they have other plans in mind; like getting me stripped down, and eating food off me, while inserting food into my vagina. The little appetite I had, vanishes with the thought of food entering my system in a completely wrong way.

Soon after the appetizers are served, Devora shows up, saving me from my frightening thoughts. I couldn't have been happier for having her, a fearless woman as my comrade while surrounded by unpredictable and vile men.

She looks happier and more relaxed. Exactly the look Ace and his employees guarantee to plaster on their clients' faces. Her eyes sweep Edward from head to toe as they shake hands, and she has the guts to do it openly without the need to hide her intense examination. I see a little smirk on her lips as if she's already given him a rating, and I'm dying to know what rating Edward got from her.

"I can't say nice to meet you, Mr. Neuberger, because we met before. I was part of the Honors program at the Board of Immigration Appeals for three years, about thirteen years ago after graduating from Columbia Law. You'd just taken up your duties as Attorney General at that time," Devora says, clearly upset by not being recognized.

How gratifying to see there are women out there who can put even powerful men in their place.

"I apologize for my terrible memory, Mrs. Vasilyev," Edward says, and he sounds indeed regretful for his mistake. Honestly, he could have easily avoided this mistake if he had his assistant run a quick Wikipedia search on the Minister and his wife. "Please enlighten us as to how we could lose such a brilliant employee to competition?" Yeah, right, Mr. Attorney General, like sucking up to her will get you anywhere.

"Do you mean to Russia as your competition?" Devora laughs; even her laughter has classiness to it. "I wasn't planning to go back to my parents' Motherland, but Demyan convinced me that I'd be better off in Russia than having to juggle with a half-successful career in the States as an attorney, and it seems he wasn't completely wrong." She takes her place next to Demyan, right across from me, and mouths her thank-you to me. She licks her lips discreetly, I guess, to show me the deliciousness of the few minutes she spent with JJ. Smiling, I shake my head at her bluntness.

Rolling her eyes at me now, she focuses her attention to the glass of liqueur in front of her. I've lost count of the amount of alcohol she's drunk, but she looks sober as if it is only plain OJ she's been drinking all this time.

Demyan and Edward take over the conversation about politics in Russia and USA, while Devora and Michael join occasionally, and when they do, it's mostly to make a humorous remark to uplift the heavy and mostly boring atmosphere in the room.

Ace eats his food silently, and I dare take secret glances at him and see his face shine brightly when our gazes meet. Vas and Pavlo seem to be bored and are unsuccessful at their attempts to hide it. Particularly Vas with his unsuccessful efforts to conceal successive yawns with the firm pressing of his lips. Like Devora, they find solace in alcohol and ask for a refill each time the servers walk around to offer more drinks.

As the dinner ends with the last sips of our dessert wines, Demyan reminds Michael of the importance in inspecting the project.

I have this nagging feeling that they won't take me to the project sightseeing and that I'll miss a crucial piece of information by not being able to see exactly what part of the project is relevant to their secret visit that made them come all the way from Russia. How can I convince Michael to take me with them? It's not like I have the tricks of an undercover agent to get myself secretly into the vehicle that they'll drive in, yet it seems more plausible than trying to persuade Michael to include me.

Devora excuses herself to the restroom again, but this time I don't think she'll pay a second visit to JJ, so I accompany her after receiving Michael's discreet nod to my request to leave. Although I know practically nothing about Devora, she seems to be my only option to get some information. She seems to be the kind of person who is motivated by money and power, but I can't picture her as demeaning as Michael. The fact that she is a woman helps a bit with my trust issues.

While Devora is in the stall, I pace up and down the restroom, trying to come up with the best way to open up to her. She may tell on me to Michael and that'd be the end of my spying activities for eternity.

Devora eyes me curiously as she leaves the stall and heads for the sinks. "Is everything okay?"

"Nothing is okay, but you know it already," I reply. "Michael has been keeping his daughter prisoner for a while now. Ace says he hurt her terribly, beat her up in front of her fiancé the last time he saw her about a week ago. He fears she'll attempt to commit suicide after Michael's tortures. Please, please, help me locate her. It's not for me. It's to save her. I don't know who else to ask for help. Everyone is working for him. I know that you're doing business with him, and I have no intentions to endanger that, but if you know where he's keeping Chloe, please tell me so we can save her."

"Oh, dear. I would tell you where she is, if I knew it." Devora washes her hands slowly and then turns around to face me. "Seriously though, I'm regretting getting into a deal with him. The worst part is that it was me who persuaded Demyan to do business with Michael. I keep hearing rumors about him trying to sell our product to some Saudi sheik. I swear if the deal doesn't go through, Demyan will not just divorce me, but also exile me from Russia."

"Did you just say Saudi sheik?" I ask with a rather high-pitched squeak, remembering the two Arabian visitors at Michael's office during the week. "Look, what I am about to say is not made up to gain your trust but is completely true. I saw two Arabian guys in Michael's office on Tuesday afternoon. Michael wasn't there but his secretary attended to them while they were visiting, and at the end of their visit one of them said, and I'm quoting, 'Tell Mr. Hawkins that we would be very pleased to do business with him.'"

"Damn it. I knew it. I saw it coming." Devora lifts her hand to rub her forehead and starts walking up and down the bathroom just like I did a minute ago. "Why else would he have Saudi visitors if not for selling —" She stops short, perhaps sensing my heightened curiosity. "Look, I can't tell you anything about the deal we have with Michael. That's like a national secret if you know what I mean. But if what you're telling me is indeed true, I might help you find Michael's daughter."

"I swear on my dead parents' graves that I'm not lying. Please, help us."

She lifts her hands up, palms against me. "All right, all right. I'll see what I can do."

I stifle the urge to run forward and hug her to show my gratitude. Even if she's doing it for all the wrong reasons, ones other than being helpful to a person in danger, if she can help me out, I will raise her to the top of the list of the women I admire.

I open the door for her, feeling obliged to serve her every way I can, and walk beside her in the long hall. As we're about to turn the corner, Devora holds up her arm in front of me to stop me and lifts her finger to her lips, urging me to keep silent. She's gesturing with her head toward the corner.

I stop short in full-panic mode and focus my attention in the direction she's pointing toward. But rather than seeing something, I just hear murmurs. Instinctively, we lean closer to the corner but not leaning out so far to get caught. When I pay close attention, I hear Edward Neuberger and an unfamiliar man's voice.

"Bring something with Desflurane. He doesn't do well on Chloroform," I hear Edward saying and nudge at Devora's arm to ask if she understands what they're talking about just with my gestures.

She leans down and whispers to my ear, "Desflurane and Chloroform are used for general anesthesia through inhalation."

"Why would he be talking about general anesthesia?"

"I don't know what impression you have of

me, but I don't read minds," Devora says with a joking tone. "It's very unsettling though."

The disgust in my stomach rises at the possibility of Michael or Edward using anesthesia on Chloe to keep her unconscious while torturing her, but no. He clearly said 'he'. That discovery, however, still isn't enough to keep me calm, because it smells terribly of malice.

"I'll need at least two men to keep him in line if he protests," Edward adds. "Make sure that they'll keep their mouths shut. I don't want anyone hearing about it, or else you'll have to deal with the consequences."

Devora shakes her head with disapproval on her face. "Men and their violent ways. Will they ever figure out there are better ways other than violence to deal with problems?"

"Exactly my thoughts."

As soon as Edward and his man leave, Devora grabs me by my elbow. "Come on. We took too long. Demyan will get suspicious that I'm testing the Pleasure Extraordinaire services." She adds a contagious smile to her comment and urges me to hurry.

As Devora suspected, Demyan eyes her

suspiciously as we enter the suite and says something in Russian. I don't understand what he's said, but Devora responds to him with a giggle and sneaks her arms around his waist to give him a kiss. With that, the angry expression on Demyan's face is replaced with a smile, and he calls his two brothers.

Michael, meanwhile, completely ignores me and Ace's existence and is busy talking with Edward. Taking advantage of my brief freedom, I find Ace arranging the stage and wink at him. Considering our fears, the first part of the evening has gone quite well. For one, no men took sexual advantage of the girls here, including me.

"How are you doing?" I ask, carefully holding the urge inside me to give him a kiss. He straightens, looking down at me with lustful eyes, pushing back his shoulders to show me the endless chest of his, and my insides begin melting. Show off.

"Not bad, except for the pain in the ass Edward Neuberger," he whispers.

"I didn't know Michael had friends among politicians, but why am I even surprised. Do you know why he is here?"

"He's Michael's lover."

I freeze with shock but move my eyes toward Edward to get a quick look at him. Not a quick look actually, because I start analyzing him as if I've seen him for the first time. Unfortunately for me, Edward notices my stare and glances back at me with a cold smile attached to his lips. I immediately return my gaze to Ace. "I had no idea he was Michael's lover."

"Be very careful around him. He's into all sorts of crime: drugs, human trafficking, blackmail," Ace says in an almost inaudible voice.

"Sounds like a man Michael would fall for."

"You got that part right. They've been together for as long as I can remember."

"Do you know where they're going now?"

Ace shakes his head no.

"I've got a feeling they're heading to the construction site. Devora mentioned a product they're going to buy from Michael, but I have no idea how that product might be related to the construction. Ugh, I could just kill someone to figure out what this whole twisted plot is about."

"Calm down." He hushes me with his index

finger on his lips. "We'll find it out sooner or later. I take it you won't be accompanying Michael?"

"I'd be lucky if he took me with him. At least I would get a chance to find out more about his plans."

He takes a cautious step toward me, still keeping a safe distance though, and casts his scorching eyes at me. "I'd be lucky if I took you to my office now and spread your legs wide over my desk."

I respond to his advance with a sharp intake of breath and a low-key squirm. Despite the stress and the potential dangers ahead, Ace's words lower my guard and make my inside muscles clench reflexively. Particularly because he did actually spread me open on his desk with some mouth-watering results.

"Devora promised to help us find Chloe," I say in an attempt to avert my focus and his to something else other than the sexual need we have for each other.

"Is that true? I guess I owe JJ a thank-you for getting into her, both literally and figuratively." He winks and drops his gaze on my torso, well, below my torso. Between my legs to be exact.

"Stop flirting with me. It's not the time."

"I don't care about the time. I need you, baby. It's hard being around you and not being able to ..." He doesn't finish his sentence with words but his seductive stare conveys the unspoken words.

"Not being able to what?" I ask feeling light-headed with all Ace's flirts in addition to the stress I've had to deal with. "Not being able to hold my hand? Not being able to tell me how gorgeous I am?"

"Those and more. Much more..." He widens his eyes with effect, his smile more dangerous than the entire group of men ahead of us.

I allow the powerful shudder his presence is causing to go through my body but keep my mouth shut to keep the forceful moan inside. My brain shuts down and resigns from all logical processes. I can't think straight even if I wanted to.

Michael and his threats? Who was he again?

Ace is making me crazy for him. I'm like a drug addict and need my Ace-fix so I can get my brain back. "You'll have to wait until later. It'll be dangerous if we both disappear at the same time."

"You're playing hard to get, lady. But I won't fall for those games." He gathers the mic and the other equipment in the cases and together with a waiter, carries them out.

I walk around the suite, unsure what to do. Michael seems to be busy with Edward; the Russian guests are in a deep discussion about God knows what. I remember having not called Taylor although she made me promise to call her before the evening. It's long past the evening hours now.

I retrieve my purse from my chair by the dinner table, glance at Michael, and when he looks back at me, I lift my hand up to my ear and make a phone call sign. He simply nods his permission and resumes his attention back on his dear Edward.

I can't believe he's being so civil about everything today. It's like the Michael who blackmailed me last week was a product of my imagination. But the reality is dark and unforgiving. He's probably putting on a good face for the sake of his guests and will show his real side, the evil one, whenever things don't go as he planned.

The Shocker

I lock the door that separates Ace's office from the attached bedroom to have some privacy as I call Taylor. She's at her sister-in-law's, Adriana's place for a dinner party but doesn't sound exactly thrilled by it. She keeps our conversation brief in order not to attract Adriana's attention and ends the call with the promise to call me tomorrow with the details.

I lean back against the door, feeling grateful the evening I was dreading all week has turned out to be actually a nice get-together. The guests haven't done anything outrageous, and to my surprise, Devora was a delight to be around. She might even provide me with information to help rescue Chloe and end this mystery behind Michael's games.

If everything goes smoothly and Chloe is free again, I'm going to lock myself and Ace into a hotel room and won't let him out for a full week of non-stop indulgence until I have my fill of him. My sex throbs with the thoughts of the hot encounters I had with him until now, and I feel those were just appetizers in comparison to what I have in mind for him in our Michael-free times.

The high levels of adrenaline running in my blood due to the stress of the evening must be causing me to have such high levels of arousal. I wonder if I'll cool down and become my boring self again when —if—I leave all the drama behind.

I reach down and squeeze myself between my legs. I seriously need to be filled with Ace's cock to take the edge away. I'll wait for him here and surprise him for a quick love session. It'll help us both focus on the important things ahead.

I unzip my dress half way, slide out of my bra, and zip it up back again. My nipples poke out immediately through the soft satin of the dress. I won't be able to take off my dress because of the time limitations but I want Ace's hands on my nipples without the barrier of the push-ups. I slip my fingers beneath the seam of my panties, over my clit, enjoying the tingles building up with my touch, and tease myself around my entrance. I'm worked up just with my fantasies and my fingers, how much more will Ace's able hands and lips drive me crazy?

My heart skips a beat when I hear Ace's office door open, and I almost unlock the deadbolt but come to a sudden halt as a man starts talking. Edward.

I pull my hand down and push it against the door together with my ear to hear what he's talking about, unable to believe this is the second time I'm eavesdropping on him in less than an hour.

"Long time no see," Edward says. *"Apparently you make it your mission to avoid being seen with Michael publicly."*

Before I can even wonder who he's talking to, Ace replies. *"That's definitely not my intention. My work keeps me pretty busy. I have no off hours, no weekends as you can guess, due to the nature of the business I'm running here at Pleasure Extraordinaire."*

"I hear your business has turned out to be a success. It'd be a pity if it ends up as a failure," Edward says.

"Why would it end up as a failure?" Ace echoes my thoughts. Why indeed? As long as the economy stays more or less stable, and the employees are dedicated to their work, Pleasure Extraordinaire should stay as a money-making machine. Unless, of course, an outsider deliberately tries sabotage it.

"I'd hate to see it ruined, but even the most successful ventures can go downhill one day," Edward says, and I can easily picture his menacing face accompanying his discouraging words. He sure doesn't mean to warn Ace to be careful with his business and make wise decisions. *"I'm sure you've heard how Berensons lost their country club within months. They thought it was a sure thing, made hundreds of thousands of dollars from it for generations, but couldn't prevent its collapse."*

Just as I expected, he's indirectly threatening Ace, bullying him perhaps to squeeze money out of him, like the Mafia does.

"We all know Michael had something to do with the end of the Berensons Club," Ace answers, sounding casual.

"That's precisely what I meant. Be careful who you're dealing with, or you might end up filing for bankruptcy."

"I'm a little lost here. What exactly are you trying to say?" Ace asks, impatience written all over in his words.

"You want me to be clear? I will be clear," Edward says. *"I want to use the services you provide here, and I want it to be you who pleases me sexually."*

My hands reach up the deadbolt with the desire to grab Edward by his collar and punch him in the face. How dare he threaten my man to get him to submit to Edward sexually? Ace is his lover's son, for fuck's sake. Doesn't that mean anything?

I stop myself as soon as I hear Ace yell, *"What? This business is only for men wanting women and women wanting men, in case you haven't noticed, and I most certainly don't work as an escort. You surely don't know what you are talking about."*

"I know what I am talking about. You seem to have forgotten our past. Let me remind you how well you served me as a little kid. Don't you remember how much you and I enjoyed each other's company during those young years of your life?"

My body shakes with a sizeable amount of bile rising up in my throat. Did Edward sexually abuse Ace as a kid? Oh, God, his nightmares. Ace mentioned he dreamed of being suffocated. Was he remembering bits and pieces of the trauma he had experienced while being raped by Edward? This is outrageous. How old was he? How can someone find a little child sexually attractive, let alone force him into sex? What kind of beasts am I dealing with? One kidnaps his own daughter; the other one molests his lover's kid. What's wrong with this world? Wherever I turn, I see dirt and ugliness.

Ace as a little child, all sweet and innocent appears in front of my eyes. How someone can even think about hurting a kid is beyond my comprehension.

Didn't Michael notice it? Perhaps he knew it all along and pretended not to have seen anything.

And worst of it all, Edward very likely will win the elections, and then even go up as high as the presidency. Will our future lie in the hands of a child molester?

I don't hear any sound, not even a creak or footsteps. What must Ace be thinking? Have the memories started coming back? How old was he when he was exposed to one of worst things a child can experience, if not the worst? My beautiful man. He has seen life in its ugliest form from early on. Lost his mother to suicide, had to watch his sister being beaten up, been beaten up himself, and this too. That's too much. Just one of those has the power to push someone into inescapable depression; he had to go through them all. As a child, no less.

I wish there were a peephole for me to see what's going on on the other side of the door. For all I know, Ace went into shock and that bastard Edward is taking advantage of his unconsciousness. I decide to mentally count until ten and if I hear no sound, I'll burst inside. I don't care if the most wanted criminal is waiting inside. I have to be with Ace.

"That's insane. I don't remember a thing," I finally hear Ace speaking. *"You didn't touch me*

really, did you? You're just talking bullshit to make a point. I'll never find you or any other man sexually attractive. And definitely not as a child. If you really did anything to me, I'll sue you."

"Please, go ahead and do it. You'll lose your business and your credibility in a matter of hours. Not just that, I'll make sure your sister and your little slut suffer in ways they haven't even thought of. Is that what you want? You'll end up being a gigolo, sucking men's dicks to survive instead of running a million-dollar business, without knowing what happened to your sister. If it's what you really want, just go ahead and sue me."

Ace remains silent for an eternity. I wish my phone could record the conversation from this far, but even if the recording had good quality, Edward would claim it was tampered or adulterated. Criminals and their methods. The innocent ones don't have much resistance against them when they know the system so well and can easily manipulate it to their benefits.

"What do you want from me?" Ace asks.

"Like I said earlier. I want to have you for myself for a few hours and it'll stay as a secret between us."

"I can't do that."

I hear the legs of a chair scratching against the floor and footsteps follow. *"Well then, feel free to expect the worst. I know where Michael keeps Chloe. She's been in great condition so far, in comparison to what I'm planning to do with her if you decline my request."*

"Please, leave her alone." Ace's words come out as a whisper. Is he crying? Very likely. I can easily picture how lost he must be feeling. Just like I did last week when Michael threatened to hurt my own sister if I didn't obey him. I can't believe the exact scenario is playing out for Ace too. Michael and Edward are truly a perfect match for each other, both using people's weaknesses to get what they want. It doesn't matter how decadent their desires are.

"I'll gladly do that, if you spare a couple of hours for me in the morning. Michael and his crew will be gone. You and I can revive the lustful times we shared in the past. I'll be here at ten on the dot. If you don't show up, I'll have my men take care of your sister."

The door of Ace's office bangs shut, and I assume Edward has exited. I'm so shocked and full of rage, I can't move a limb. Ace doesn't know I've been hiding out here, eavesdropping on probably the most repulsive conversation of his life. I want to seek him out and embrace him to remind him I'm with him in this, that he doesn't have to fight alone. However, what can I do? I'm here because I'm trapped in the exact same situation by Michael. He will most likely choose the same decision I did. Go with the flow and follow the orders of the evil to protect his loved ones.

I can't look him in the eye and see the hurt, the hopelessness, the degradation. Seeing me won't do any good for him either. His pride must be bruised; his confidence in himself—in everything—ruined. Is there a way out of this?

A loud thud behind the door startles me, and I have no explanation for that noise. Unlocking the deadbolt slowly, I open the door to see the entire content of Ace's desk, including his desktop and laptop, on the floor, but he's nowhere to be seen. Where has he gone? What's he going to do?

I have to do something, and I know whom I can ask help from although Ace will hate me for this. I get my phone out and dial Zane.

The inevitable

"You're a wise woman to turn to me for help," Zane says as I nod at his bodyguard before closing the door of the Summer Suite against him, hoping he won't eavesdrop on my conversation with Zane. "I've been working on a plan to destroy Michael for a long time. I was going to start my campaign in a week, but I can start it tomorrow to help you out."

"Oh, my God. Really? That'll be fantastic." I turn around to face him, excited and nervous in equal parts. He has the power to help Ace, Chloe, and me out of this mess.

"But it won't be for free. I want something in exchange." Zane hums letting his eyes sweep me up and down, and I'm starting to guess what he might want in exchange. Oh, no! "I want to re-live that afternoon in your apartment. I want you weak and wet for me. I want to feel you convulse around my cock while you scream my name."

"Please, don't ask me for that. I can't ... I can't do it," I say when I turn around and stroll to the center of the suite. When I was contemplating the worst that might happen to me with the Russian guests, how could I know the real degradation would come from Zane, the guy who promised to help me against Michael? Why can't he just help me out without asking for anything in return?

"Why not? You had the hots for me before. Remember?" He takes a step toward me, furrowing his eyebrows and widening his eyes in an angry, hostile way. "Are you saying I just imagined how you flirted with me the first time we met, then at the lunch? If I'd thought you had no interest in me, I wouldn't have signed up to pleasure you as an escort."

Oh, we all know why you signed up to pleasure me. I keep that thought hidden at the back of my mind, though, and remain silent.

"I'm sure I wasn't wrong with my assumption," Zane continues. "You wanted me as much as I wanted you. That's why you didn't turn me down when I came to your apartment unannounced. Isn't that true?"

"It is. Well, it was, but now I don't feel anything for you." I lace my hands together, tilting my head down to look at them, and realize I'm without a bra and my nipples are clearly outlined through the thin satin fabric of the dress.

He walks around me slowly, evaluating me, then stops right in front of me. "Don't tell me it's Ace."

I remain silent. That should be enough for an answer for him.

"What? Did you fall in love with him in ... what ... two weeks?" he asks, laughing.

I'd laugh at myself if someone had told me I would, before I personally experienced it. But it's true. Sort of. I'm not sure what I feel for Ace is as strong as love, but it's there nevertheless and makes me feel disinterested in other men.

Zane lifts his hand, crooks the index finger, and runs it along my throat, and tilts my chin up. My skin tingles with his touch. Our gazes meet, and I feel his eyes sparkle. "That's okay. I'm happy to help you realize your feelings for Ace are only temporary."

"I really don't want to have sex with you," I whisper slowly, hoping his ego won't be hurt. But what man's ego wouldn't be hurt after hearing those pearls of words out of a woman's mouth?

"That's a pity, then there's really no incentive for me to change my original plan. Ace will just have to deal with the cock in his ass by himself."

He can't be seriously okay with a man's intentions to try and rape his brother. There's no way he is that evil. If he is indeed, it makes him drop lower in standing in my eyes, making it even more impossible for me to sleep with him willingly.

"Is that what you want, baby?" he asks. "Edward raping Ace? Don't you think he molested him enough as a child? Will you allow him to take advantage of Ace again?"

"You knew he was being molested?"

"Of course I did. I witnessed it when we were

kids. Edward made me promise not to say a word about it, but I told my mother anyway. She tried to protect Ace as much as she could, but Edward had his way around our house. He stopped only when Mom threatened him to tell everything to Michael. But I guess his obsession with Ace hasn't diminished after all these years."

"You can save him now. You don't want him getting hurt. Do you?"

He shrugs, indifferent as if we're talking about a random topic and not his brother's dignity. "He was a kid back then, helpless and harmless. It's different now. He is an adult, he can take care of himself."

"No, he can't. He needs your help. Please."

"I don't get into deals that I don't get anything out of."

Just like his father. "Your sister's safety isn't reason enough for you?" I ask. "Edward can hurt her before you know it."

"Not if Ace complies with him, and from the looks of it he will. Sorry, but you'll have to find another way." He turns around, heading toward the door.

Oh my god. He can't be serious. He's bluffing

to get into my pants.

Or?

Zane approaches the door and holds the doorknob. If he leaves, he won't come back. He opens the door hastily and steps out. That doesn't look like a bluff.

"Wait. I'll do it." *I'll fucking let you fuck me.*

He turns around to face me, his eyebrows lifted. "I'm not sure if I want to have sex with a woman who'll do it as a chore and not out of desire."

"What do you want now?" I let out a loud breath to show my frustration and anger.

"I want you willing and aroused for me."

"Okay, I will be." I won't be the first woman to fake an orgasm.

"Will you really be?" He closes the door when I give him a reassuring nod. I unlace my hands, letting my arms fall beside my body, and push back my shoulders to give him a clear view of my hardened nipples. He smiles at my attempt and walks back to me.

His hands lift and land on my stomach, slowly making their way up toward my breasts. I swallow hard, trying to hold back the feeling of disgust at the dangerous proximity of those hands to my breasts. His lips part while his eyes stare at my breasts. I'll be lucky if I can go through this without throwing up. He smiles seconds before his palms cover my breasts like a bra. The fabric in between does nothing to ease the feeling of disgust rising in the pit of my stomach. I close my eyes to at least avoid the repulsive view of the lust brewing in his eyes. He pinches at my nipples so hard I scream from the pain of it.

"Are you sure you can handle me?" he asks.

My eyes snap open, and I can hardly move my lips. "Yes."

"Look. I'll know if you fake it, and the deal will be off as if we didn't have sex. Do you really want me?" He flattens his hands on my breasts and moves them up and down.

Why do you have to ask? Just do what you want and get out of my life, you asshole. I don't voice that thought and instead nod like a good girl.

"Does it turn you on to kneel in front of me and take my cock inside your mouth?"

I nod.

"Answer me."

"Yes, it does."

"You can't fucking lie. But I see you're trying. And lucky for you, I'm great in bed. So let's give it a try."

"What, here?" I ask.

"Did you want to go somewhere else?" His hands are still on my chest, kneading my breasts.

"Yeah, somewhere where Ace can't see us."

"Do you want to hide it from him? No, honey. Part of my satisfaction will come from the possibility that he'll witness this. Perhaps you haven't heard about the little incident that happened between me and Ace. He stole my girlfriend a few years ago. I watched him fuck her, and I'll be damned if I let him get away with that."

"But he had no idea she was your girl. She approached him first."

"Doesn't matter about the details. It still fucking hurts."

"I can't do anything with you, knowing he can burst in at any second," I admit.

"Oh, he will burst in and try to get you away from me. But you'll stay and let him watch while my cock drives you to your orgasms. That's what this whole deal is about."

"You're a sadist."

"So?" He lowers one hand down to my belly and lands it on my mound. "I want this moist and climaxing. Here and now."

"This is insane."

"Do we have a deal or not? I don't have the entire night." He crooks his fingers and cups my sex through the skirt of my dress and I flinch back.

I'll let him have sex with me while I fake an orgasm. Yes, I can handle that and more if it'll save Ace from Edward's plans.

I reach up and wrap my hands around his neck to pull him in for a kiss as an answer. I can do this. I was preparing to have sex with total strangers. Zane is nothing compared to the horror of being fucked by Demyan in front of half a dozen spectators. Zane is no stranger to my body. Closing my eyes helps in addition to my self-suggestions to push down the lump of disgust in my throat.

I should remember the excitement Zane's presence stirred up in my body that afternoon. I desired him not long ago. I can desire him now too. My skin should sizzle with his touch, his kiss. Oh, shit, he's sticking his tongue deep inside my mouth without any warming up. His torso is pressed against me, and I can feel his hardness between us. My heart races, but for all the wrong reasons. There's no way I can bite down my gag reflex. I jerk back, pushing him away from me, and cover my mouth, trying to inhale deeply to calm my stomach.

"You gotta be kidding me. This can't be happening," Zane yells.

"I'm so sorry." I wipe my mouth with the back of my hand, embarrassment stopping me from looking up at his eyes.

"The deal is off. Find someone else to save your boyfriend." Zane swings around and leaps toward the door.

Oh, God, what do I do now? How can I make it better? There has to be a way. Suddenly an idea pops up in my mind, and I run and stand between him and the door before he can reach for the handle. "Please, give me some time."

His jaw tightens. He shakes his head now, his expression cold and menacing.

"You want me to orgasm, don't you? Is that what you want? You want me to cum while having sex with you?"

He rolls his eyes, I guess, for stating the obvious. "It's too late."

"Give me another chance. It'll be fantastic."

"I doubt it."

I start toward him until our bodies touch, lift my hands up on his torso, and stand on my toes to move close to his mouth. Our lips brush when I say, "You'll have me soaking wet and crazy for some hard, sweaty sex."

He takes a sharp breath and then exhales it through his lips, radiating warmth to my mouth. I lick my lips and leave a soft kiss on his. It's not too bad. Not stomach-churning like his forceful tongue down in my throat. "Give me a sec," I say and reach for the phone attached on the wall beside the door.

I sense Zane eyeing me suspiciously as I talk to the boy at the front desk, "Hi. I'm at the Summer Suite. Can you send Laila over, please? Tell her Seven needs her help."

"Laila?" Zane asks. I can see he's astonished; his eyebrows lift and his jaw drops. I surprised myself too. Of all people, Laila will be my savior through this Zane challenge.

"Laila," I repeat.

"I'm not fucking another woman."

"You won't be."

I start toward him, working hard to recall the emotions running wild in me for Zane, before Ace claimed them all for himself. Establishing he's a good-looking man isn't hard at all. Tall, masculine, powerful, with daring green eyes and teasing lips. He had pleasured me with those lips to my utmost satisfaction. He forced an orgasm out of me with ease. Why shouldn't they work their magic now too? All I need to do is focus on Laila while Zane takes what he wants from me.

He's unsure and cautious, not risking touching me for fear of inducing another urge to throw up out of me. I should be glad that he's not forcing me into it like the way other men would do. He wants me to enjoy it as much as he will. That in itself is both good and bad. Good, because I won't feel like I'm being raped; bad, because he will use it to hurt Ace.

Inhaling a long, deep breath, I resume my hands back on his chest, aware that now there's no going back. Zane will have me and most likely Ace will witness it. Oh, God, I can live with the having-sex-with-Zane part, but I don't know if I can live through seeing the letdown on Ace's face if he sees us.

Zane studies my face with wonder as if he has seen me for the first time. "I'm not sure if it will work."

"Why shouldn't it? You, me, and another hot girl. Weren't you the one who suggested having me with one of your girlfriends? This won't be any different."

The hardness on his face is slowly replaced with his patented 'Let's get physical' expression, the side of his lip curling up, his eyes narrowed, promising all the dirty things he'll do to me.

A knock on the door, and I find myself hurrying to open it. I shouldn't think of the upcoming minutes as horrible or there's no way I can fulfil his requirement and the deal will go off.

Laila stands at the doorway wearing a black lacey robe. I can see the outlines of the bra, panties, and the garter belt. To be honest, I can't wait for her to get rid of the robe and explore her body.

She smiles a beautiful, friendly smile and winks at me. "I'm glad you wanted to see me again."

I guess I was the only one denying her effect

on me, and I'm grateful she's not repulsed by my special interest. "Thanks for coming. I assume you know ..." Shall I introduce Zane with his name or his nickname?

"Big Boy." Zane comes forward and catches her hand to kiss it. Oh, he's going to enjoy Laila too. "I saw you before, but never had the pleasure to introduce myself." The hungry way Zane eyes Laila tells me I've just discovered the antidote to his promiscuity.

"Laila." Laila giggles softly and fluffs her hair behind her shoulder with a quick move of her hand.

I scan the suite to locate a stereo and push the play button. As a soft, sensual tune starts, Laila walks in the middle of the room with all the self-confidence a beautiful woman can have and shrugs out of her robe. The bra, tight against her breasts, makes them double their real size, but it's the garter belt that's making my heart hop. It's a four-inch black lace that starts right above her ass crack, and the thong she's wearing is a thin line that's lost between the round cheeks of her ass. A sight to behold both for men and women.

Zane walks behind her, like a tiger after his prey, and settles on the edge of the bed, spreading his legs wide apart for us to see his hard-on bulging through his slacks.

"Why don't you lose that dress too?" Zane asks me, and I find myself not really bothered by the prospect of getting naked in front of an audience. All thanks to Laila, I assume.

Both Laila and Zane watch me intently as I unzip my dress slowly and turn my back against them so they can enjoy the full assets of my buttocks. Zane must be comparing my ass with Laila's. I'm not sure whose he'll choose if he had to. He'll probably go with both.

Since the dress is tight around my body, it takes some time to peel out of it. When it's finally tossed on the floor, I cover my naked breasts with my hands and turn to face Zane. I'm only in a black thong and black pumps. No high-thighs or garter belt to tone my body, but Zane looks at me with the same appetite as he has Laila. He points at my arms, telling me to reveal my breasts without words. I shake my head playfully and walk in slow steps toward them.

Laila reaches out for my hands and pushes them down. I feel heat surging toward my face with shame when she runs her delicate hands on my nipples. So different from the rough touches of a man. I feel moisture pooling up between my legs as she plays with my breasts. I can tell she's enjoying it too.

I seriously don't want her to stop massaging my breasts, but she does. She drops her hands to grab mine and lifts them to her own breasts hiding behind her bra. When I feel the fullness of the round globes beneath my palms, I finally grasp the obsession of men with breasts. Pulling down her bra, I roll her nipples between my fingers and watch her moan and throw her head back with pleasure.

"This is so much better than I expected," Zane says a few feet away from us. "Come here," he orders, and Laila slips her arm around my waist as we walk to Zane. I help Laila out of her bra and the panties, but she keeps her garter belt and the nylons on. Zane pushes his knees further apart and pulls me between them, my sex toward him. Slowly he pulls my panties down and runs his thumb from my mound down my clit to my entrance.

His eyes widen as my wetness covers the tip of his finger. "You're wet all right." He grins up at me and sticks his tongue out to moisten his lips. Laila stands by my side, very close to me. I dare not turn to face her for the fear of getting kissed by her. I enjoy her sensuality, but I'm not sure about sharing a kiss with her.

Zane pulls my hips closer to his face and I know what's coming. A part of me wishes to put an end to this charade, but the other part demands to re-live the forcefulness of his lips on me. His lips touch me first, capturing my clit. Before my body can even register the shock of his rough mouth, he digs his finger into my core, earning a moan from me.

Laila's hands on my breast and back boost the intense feeling exponentially. She leans in and brushes her lips against mine, kneading them softly, gently and occasionally licking them with her tongue. Again, it's very different than a kiss from a man, but my brain is slowly shutting off to get into details of a comparison as my sex is roughened up by Zane's finger and lips.

I find my hand grabbing Zane's arm to push him deeper inside me and hear him laugh against my flesh. I'm allowing another man inside my body and enjoying it shamelessly while loving another man. What does that say about me? No. I can't allow logic to rule me, or Zane will notice and drop everything. This isn't for my pleasure although I'm enjoying it. It's for Ace. For his safety.

Just when Zane picks up the speed of his finger inside me, he withdraws it out of the blue, and pulls back. My body moves forward to him in response to get his hands and lips back on me, but in vain, because he's looking up at me and shaking his head teasingly. I hate being played like that. He wants me to orgasm but denies me one when I get very close to it.

Laila pulls back too and kneels down in front of Zane to help him out of his shirt and pants. She's a pro at not letting her emotions get ahead of her to allow all parties to enjoy each other.

Now fully naked, Zane leans further back on the bed, resting on his elbows. His long cock is a menacing sight, but arousing too, to my utter astonishment. Now the memories of it sliding into me in my apartment come back with vivid details. It's sick to think of him sexually while my heart belongs to his brother. I'd stop everything this very minute if he let me go.

"Sit on it," he says, and for a second I'm confused if he means Laila or me. Laila moves ahead and straddles him, her back against him and her face toward me. My mouth goes dry at the sight of her sex gliding forward and backward against Zane's long cock.

"You're good," Zane spanks Laila's back and grabs her hips to move her faster against his member. Laila moans, biting her lower lip.

"Lick my balls," Zane orders, this time clearly for me. I've never been fond of licking a man's balls, but at least his are shaved. I kneel in front of them and place my hands on his thighs and dig my head down. The scent of Laila's sex hits my nostrils, and I notice the wetness on Zane's cock. She runs her hands through my hair as I start licking Zane's balls. They're very dry and like I expected, not really enjoyable to lick.

Zane lifts Laila up holding her hips, and I watch as the head of his penis sinks inside Laila's vagina. She doesn't take all of him inside at first and just continues teasing herself with the head for some minutes. Zane doesn't look like he can hold out for her to play another minute and pushes his hips up so his penis is buried all the way inside her. I have to move a few inches back to give them space as Zane fucks her. This is the second time I'm witnessing Laila having sex, and both times with men that I enjoyed too.

"Keep sucking my balls," Zane yells between

his ragged breaths as Laila works him up. I resume my position between his legs, but it's hard to follow their rhythm while Zane moves his hips up and down and Laila moves forward and backward. Despite the big size of his penis, his balls are small and make me wonder how big Ace's balls are. I should pay closer attention to them next time. If there is a next time at all. Particularly if he shows up now and watches me getting intimate with Zane.

Laila's skills don't stop amazing me. She's full of energy and enthusiasm as she bounces up and down on top of Zane, and Zane's face tells me this will be one of the shortest sexual encounters of his life. An embarrassingly short time for an ordinary guy, but even worse for a professional escort like himself.

Will the deal be off if he comes now? It shouldn't because he willingly chose Laila over me, and if he can't control his ejaculation, it's his problem. But, I shouldn't completely ignore the possibility that he might want to take a break and then go for a second round. He might even ask me to suck his penis, which is now coated with Laila's juices. As much as I find Laila sexy, I'm not sure I can turn off my gag reflex when I have to taste her on the cock of a man that I despise.

My tongue starts feeling numb with all the licking on Zane's unwanted area, not to forget the weird position giving me a neck ache. Laila speeds up, earning loud moans from Zane. He's a goner for sure. I can't imagine a man who can handle that kind of performance longer.

"Slow down, sexy. Let's leave some for Seven too," Zane mumbles the words I've been afraid to hear. Laila stops short and looks up at me, the hazed expression on her face turning worried. She must have been aware of what's going on between Ace and me, and that's why she was her best, but even she can't prevent what's about to come. The moment of truth has arrived, and I have no more options left to turn to.

Ace's words echo in my head, *"You won't fuck another man, single or married. You're now mine."* The memory of that special moment hurts every cell in my body as I stare at Zane.

He slides out of Laila and holds his penis, rubbing it up and down. "Come now," he orders. I know what I should do, what I will do, but it still gives me pain. He'll fuck me, mark me, even make me orgasm, and the special bond between Ace and me will vanish.

The only good that will come out of this is Zane stopping Edward and Michael without Ace witnessing the price of that favor. However, the murmurs coming from the corridor are likely proof I'm wrong. Zane straightens up and holds my hand, urging me toward his naked body. I get onto the bed on my knees and slowly lift one leg to straddle him. He grabs my hips and positions me right on top of his cock, the head of it touching my entrance.

The sounds in the corridor get louder. I close my eyes, wishing it's not Ace, and let Zane capture my lips into a rough kiss. I can't do it. I can't fucking fake enjoying Zane's sexual advances if it's Ace out there. Worse yet, if he sees me. It's not the feeling of disgust or guilt. My heart simply won't allow me to proceed with Zane's demands.

I pull away, feeling a tear fall out of my eye, and shake my head at Zane. He closes his eyes for a moment, perhaps thinking how he should maneuver. When I start to get out of his lap, he opens his eyes and drags me back to his chest. "I know why Michael hired you. I know every little detail related to that contract, and I'll tell you everything if you do as I said, like a good girl. You'll have the last piece of your puzzle, and I'll have my revenge on Ace. How about that? Can you do that much?"

I freeze, my mind going into shock with his revelation. Can he be lying? Using my weakness to his benefit? His expression doesn't reveal anything that I can use to gauge his honesty.

The door bursts open, the loud banging of it bringing me back to my senses. I don't dare turn, and I don't need to, to know it is Ace storming inside. I sit back on Zane's lap, rest one hand on his shoulder, and hold his cock with the other as he buries it deep inside me.

And I moan his name, loud and clear for everyone around to hear, "Zane."

THE END

ABOUT THE AUTHOR

Liv Bennett lives in California with her scientist husband, toddler daughter, and two loud budgies. Reading and writing erotic romance are her favorite forms of relaxation, in addition to long walks and yoga. She's a social drinker of coffee but a serious tea addict.

Sign up to get alerts about her upcoming releases

eepurl.com/F_nqD
www.facebook.com/LivBennettAuthor
slivbennett@gmail.com

*

The PURSUIT series by Liv Bennett

An Illicit Pursuit (Zach & Pat)

The Pursuit of Passion (Taylor & Adam, 1)

An Everlasting Pursuit (Taylor & Adam, 2)

Pleasure Extraordinaire 1 (Lindsay)

Pleasure Extraordinaire 2 (Lindsay)

Pleasure Extraordinaire 3 (Lindsay)

Made in the USA
Columbia, SC
26 May 2020

98479599R00143